SH
C000273490

When Carl Danning gave her the job of tracking down and interviewing the elusive Richard Kaufmann, Alix was far from pleased—but the assignment led her into helping Richard repair the situation between him and his ex-wife. If only it had helped her sort out the situation between herself and Carl!

Books you will enjoy
by MARGARET WAY

TEMPLE OF FIRE

Julian Standford had all the autocratic ways of his overbearing family. He was also rich, handsome and charming—when he wanted to be. In short, he had everything. Everything except a heart. But the only way Fleur could be with her beloved young brother again was to live in the same house with Julian and his overwhelming relatives. Could she possibly stand up to them *all*?

FLAMINGO PARK

All right, so Nick Langford had known Kendall for years and was far older and more experienced than she was—but did that give him the right to try and run her life for her? She was quite capable of looking after herself—wasn't she?

LORD OF THE HIGH VALLEY

When her fiancé Robin was killed, Rosanne felt the least she could do was agree with his stepbrother Ross's suggestion that she visit Robin's home in Queensland and try to comfort his mother. But, once there, she realised that Ross himself had nothing but contempt for her—and it was all undeserved. Why did he think so badly of her—and why did she care so much about his opinion?

THE RAINBOW BIRD

Paige Norton was visiting Koombala, the vast Benedict cattle empire in the middle of the Australian Outback, as the guest of Joel Benedict. She had looked forward to it immensely, although she hadn't much liked the sound of Joel's stepbrother Ty, the Boss of Koombala—and when she met Ty, she like the reality even less . . .

SHADOW DANCE

BY

MARGARET WAY

MILLS & BOON LIMITED

15-16 BROOK'S MEWS
LONDON W1A 1DR

All the characters in this book have no existence outside the imagination of the Author, and have no relation whatsoever to anyone bearing the same name or names. They are not even distantly inspired by any individual known or unknown to the Author, and all the incidents are pure invention.

The text of this publication or any part thereof may not be reproduced or transmitted in any form or by any means, electronic or mechanical, including photocopying, recording, storage in an information retrieval system, or otherwise, without the written permission of the publisher.

This book is sold subject to the condition that it shall not, by way of trade or otherwise, be lent, resold, hired out or otherwise circulated without the prior consent of the publisher in any form of binding or cover other than that in which it is published and without a similar condition including this condition being imposed on the subsequent purchaser.

First published 1981

Australian copyright 1981
Philippine copyright 1981
This edition 1981

© Margarent Way 1981

ISBN 0 263 73487 0

Set in 11 on 12 pt. Monophoto Baskerville

Made and printed in Great Britain by
Richard Clay (The Chaucer Press), Ltd.,
Bungay, Suffolk

CHAPTER ONE

WHEN Alix went into Carl Danning's office, he nodded curtly, then picked up the phone.

Typical Danning, she thought; deliberately keeping me waiting while he makes a perfectly unnecessary phone call. One would think he'd get tired of it. She moved quietly and sat down in one of the ultra-modern black leather armchairs that faced the huge executive desk.

These days, the Chief's office was particularly impressive, but she longed for the old suave calmness of Joe Ferguson's time. Unfortunately Joe's faintly shabby gentility had been considered as thoroughly outmoded as Joe. Both had gone. Joe and the decor.

She looked around the room appraisingly, amazed at Danning's superb taste. In the beginning, she hadn't been prepared to give him credit for anything, so it was painful to note that he could deal with every contingency. Even interiors. No decorator had been called in. He had done it all himself, evidently the kind of man who reacted to challenge. She wondered if she would ever get used to working for him. Things were so different now that Joe was gone.

The one-sided conversation continued with Danning punching home every word. He didn't even stop to draw breath, and Alix had to admit it was understandable that few people on the staff really liked him. Yet he was brilliant; the bright boy of journalism. In the little over a year since he had taken over the Chief's job, he had saved the magazine from sure death and in the process kept a lot of people in jobs. He was a professional, a complete professional with the instincts of a tiger.

In Joe's time, *Impact* had been a small but prestigious monthly magazine. 'Arty', the man on the street would have called it, and left it strictly alone. But Danning had changed all that. In the teeth of hostility and fierce opposition, he had ousted Joe and the national advertising manager and by radically expanding the format, was turning *Impact* into one of the top selling magazines in the country.

Of course they still retained the big names as feature writers, but now there was a glossy cover featuring, most often, a stunningly beautiful girl, and inside a diversity of articles on everything from the Australian aborigine to improving one's sexual performance. At any rate, no matter how one looked at it, *Impact* sold . . . and sold . . . and sold.

I'm becoming a cynic, Alix thought, and tore her glance away from a splendid abstract painting to look at Carl Danning's down-bent dark head. She never looked at him if she could help it. In fact she didn't care if he fell over and broke his neck. His hair was very thick with a crisp, deep wave. He was even good-looking in a heavyweight boxer kind of way, and so successful with women he obviously thought it only a matter of time before Alix allowed herself to be compromised. Like Sally. Thinking of Sally made her shudder in disgust. She detested men who had a callous hand with women. And Sally hadn't even been a woman, just a pretty, silly, oversexed little kid. Now

Sally and her chattering tongue had been moved on. One would think he'd have a little more discretion, if one couldn't expect principle.

She saw him shake his head impatiently and his black brows came together. He was very dark in colouring and aggressively male—frighteningly so, she thought sometimes. Now his strong fingers started to do a devil's tattoo on the desk and she could have laughed aloud at his aura of burning energy. A near genius he might be, but not a living example of decency.

He must have become aware of her piercing scrutiny, for he looked up sharply and a glint came into his coal-black eyes. Of course he knew of her antagonism, though usually she kept it hidden behind the veil of good manners. Now she sat motionless, unable to look away from him, recognising his raw power. He had it in abundance. The physical strength she disliked, the rapier-sharp brain.

Very deliberately he let his eyes move over her, brilliant with insolence. Over her shining blonde hair, neatly caught back in a clasp, over her face and slender body, down the length of legs to her elegantly shod feet.

In that moment, Alix *hated* him, but her face remained super-cool and relaxed. Carl Danning wouldn't get any reaction from her, and she knew it was a source of some irritation to him. They were forever dancing around one another, sparring partners locked in a silent war. He stared for another moment, then returned his gaze to a contract on his desk.

'To hell with him!' he said forcefully into the

phone. 'I want something new, not the usual tripe!'

But tripe sells, she thought blithely. The stuff that would have made Joe wince was proving extraordinarily popular.

'Tell him—'

Immediately Alix tuned out. Another thing she disliked about Danning; the biting earthiness of his language. Especially in front of her. It was difficult to see why he was attracted to her at all, unless it was the fun of the chase. It could be the chase was everything, and he had no use for conquest.

'Right!' He hung up the phone briskly and waved his hand with a gesture that meant *that* was settled. 'I liked the piece you did on Raylene Webb. Empty-headed little bitch, but the public seem to like her.'

'They like the image she projects,' Alix offered, surprised at the spurt of pleasure she felt at his approval. Raylene Webb was a rising young actress in a domestic soap opera, but she was nowhere near as wholesome and fresh as the character she portrayed in the series.

'Well, it was fairly obvious you were putting the words in her mouth,' he said offhandedly. 'Anyway, it was good. I've got something a whole lot tougher for you now.'

'Oh, splendid!' She said that to everything he asked, and now she realised she said it to annoy him. She *always* wanted to annoy him. Stupid really, when she desperately needed her job.

'I just hope, for your sake, you can manage it,' he returned bitingly, obviously struggling to control his irritation. He hated cool blondes. Cool, touch-me-not types with a university degree and a social background. Nothing had been handed to him on a silver platter.

Still she didn't ask him what the assignment was and he said a little harshly: 'Unless you'd prefer to be working somewhere else, you'd better pay attention.'

'But I am!' She shook her head in wonder and his smile tightened.

'Be careful, golden girl. I could sack you tomorrow.'

Of course he could. Danning would and could kick anyone out. If they didn't deliver, or they crossed him.

'Simply tell me what you want done,' she said evenly, greatly lamenting the fact that interesting, well paid jobs were hard to come by.

'That's better!' He interpreted her quiet tone as an apology and looked back at her steadily. 'I want you to get an interview with Richard Kaufmann.'

'What?' For an instant Alix was stunned by his sheer audacity. 'But it's common knowledge he sees no one.'

'Then it's about time he opened up,' he said with his usual insensitivity. 'A man like that can't expect too much of a private life. He was once a pianist of international standing and he married a great singer, even if she couldn't wait to divorce him. There ought to be a story in that.'

'I'm sure there would,' Alix agreed dryly, 'but he's refused countless interviews in the past. All the women's magazines have tried. What they say of him is true. Nowadays he's become a recluse.'

'So was Lewis Wollcott,' he pointed out crisply, 'but you got to him.'

'Actually it was a friend who engineered it.'

'Ah, yes, dear old Lady May!' he smiled a little acidly. 'It comes in handy to have friends in high places.'

'Yes, it does.' She slumped bonelessly in the chair. 'But I could never ask May to arrange an entrée for me into the Kaufmann home. She simply wouldn't do it.'

'Not even for her goddaughter?' he asked dryly. 'I must say I find that hard to believe.'

'Then you don't know May,' she said hardily. 'She's a great respecter of privacy. It was different with Lewis Wollcott. He'd been one of Mary's protégés in his early days and though he's less than enthusiastic about interviews it's mostly because he's too busy composing. Apparently the failure of his marriage upset Kaufmann deeply. I should think he'd be a deeply sensitive man.'

'And you *so* admire sensitivity!' He regarded her blandly, the tilt of his head and the set of his body inexorably mocking.

'I do,' she said firmly, 'and I couldn't possibly intrude.'

His mouth turned down jeeringly. A disturbing mouth; she didn't like it. 'But that's your job, darling. *Intruding.* But seeing you're such a lady, you do it beautifully.'

'I guess it is.' The truth of it stopped her. She shrugged and looked down at her ringless hands. Once she had been engaged, but Guy had very quickly bowed out when he found out there wasn't really any money. Charming, likeable, gutless Guy.

'What are you thinking about?' Carl Danning asked her disconcertingly.

'How do you propose I go about it?' She evaded his question with one of her own. Was he a mind-reader or something?

'Think about it,' he said sarcastically. 'You're a beautiful girl.'

'Should that mean something?'

'He had a reputation as a ladies' man.'

'So have you!' It was out before she could stop herself.

'The hell I have!' he said explosively, and his anger pervaded every inch of the room.

'Well, I'm sorry.' She made a great effort to smile. 'I'm surprised you take my comment so seriously. Why get excited?'

'Don't put any tags on me, Conroy,' he said warningly.

'Please, I was only joking.'

'And a sour one at that. But then you've been sour on me since I pushed old Joe out of the chair. Haven't you?'

'You never ask a question, just throw out challenges.'

'Then answer.'

'I was very fond of Joe,' she said defensively.

'Fergusons's little pet.'

'He was like a father to me!' Her smoky eyes darkened to slate.

'Really?' He had a good voice, an actor's voice capable of honing or shading every word.

'Yes, really,' she said a little heatedly. Bother the man, with his tasteless implications! 'He was like a father to us all.'

'Oh, bravo! He sure got *Impact* into a mess.'

'Public taste being what it is.'

'And don't knock it, girlie,' he told her relentlessly. 'It provides your bread and butter. It also sends your young brother to the same old posh school.'

'I know it.' The colour had risen under her creamy skin, lifting her cool face to real beauty. Many was the time she had wanted to tell Danning to go to hell, only for Peter. Peter was very clever. He wanted to be an architect and she didn't really know how she was going to afford it.

'Why don't you get married?' he asked her abruptly.

'Surely I would have to fall in love first?' she confronted him directly.

'What happened to that nice ex-fiancé of yours?'

'He likes heiresses,' she said, and actually smiled.

'He's a fool!' He spoke slowly, drawing out every word.

'*I* was the fool, believing him.'

'And you're over it?'

He was looking at her intently, too intently she thought, and she dropped into facetiousness. 'Surely you're not thinking of starting a column—advice to the lovelorn.'

'As it happens, that's not so terrible. Some people need advice.'

'Not you.' She gave him a brittle smile, the only kind of smile she could ever manage for him.

'Why don't we come to the point?' he returned coolly. 'You can do wonders when you try. See if you can get a story out of Kaufmann, a few photos.

Women seem to go for melancholy types. Between you and me I think it should be a very ennobling experience.'

'Perhaps,' she said lightly. 'Why didn't you favour Leo Saunders with the honour?'

'I would have thought that was obvious,' he glanced at her briefly. 'What it comes down to, Conroy, is this: a good part of your incredible success is your appearance. It suits your personality perfectly. People think they can trust you, so they open up.'

'As it happens, they can!' She flushed a little, certain she was being ribbed. 'Honesty is a very important commodity.'

'Especially in your line of work. Having a patrician face helps.' His tone implied it cut no ice with him. 'Privately I think you can manage it—and you *will* if you want a career on this magazine.'

'All right, then, I'll see what I can do.' She stood up quickly, a tall, slender girl with a clear-cut, well-bred beauty.

To her surprise, he stood up as well and came around the desk towards her. 'It must be a dreadful comedown not to have the money you were used to?'

'It's far worse not to have my parents.'

'Well, you've got guts,' he observed, seeing how the afternoon sun turned her hair into a glory. 'A lot more than I thought when we met.'

'I'm glad.' Alix grimaced a little, not caring what he thought of her. He was taller and broader than most men and she had to tilt her graceful neck just to look at him. 'By the way, when's my deadline?'

'Normally it would be the first of the month, but in this case, I'll allow you more time. I want it to go into our Christmas issue. Maybe we could even get him on the cover.'

'What a departure,' she said, midway to the door.

'Once in a while it's nice to have a change,' his voice deepened with humour. 'It's certain to appeal to the women—Byronic good looks poised over the piano, and agonised expression.'

'And what if he doesn't play ball?'

'Conroy, he's all yours!' A frown creased his forehead and he returned abruptly to his desk. 'I've got work to do.'

'Yes, *sir*!'

It was clearly dismissal, and as she went back to the office her expression was a mixture of anger and amusement.

'What's with you?' Gary Pearson asked her out of the corner of his mouth.

'A difficult assignment.'

'Enthralling, darling. Do tell.' Gary took his afternoon cup of coffee in both hands and took a great gulp.

'Not a bit of it, it's a secret.'

'You maddening girl.' He looked at her curiously as she put a sheet of paper into the typewriter.' Every time you come out of Danning's office you seem to be stretched taut.'

'That's how I feel,' she admitted.

'Surely you're not keeping up the feud?' Gary yawned wearily. 'In spite of what we all thought at the beginning he's made a damn good boss.'

'I suppose he has.' Alix looked curiously unimpressed. 'I just don't happen to like him.'

'He knows that,' Gary drank the rest of his coffee

down thirstily, 'yet he keeps you on the payroll. Ever wonder why?'

'The high standard of my work,' she suggested smilingly.

'I think he enjoys watching you.'

'What nonsense!' She stopped typing to examine Gary's puckish face.

'Why do you think dear old Val is so jealous?' he nodded his head sagely.

'I'm not even going to condescend to reply to that.' The question flurried her so much, she made a mistake.

'The truth is, my little duck, Val's got it in for you and you've got it in for Danning. Even before he arrived.'

'I think at that time, so did you,' she countered dryly.

'Well, we were all pretty fond of Joe.' Gary put his hands behind his head and leaned back in his chair. 'Funny, that, when he was putting us out of business.'

'It's impossible to please all of the people all of the time,' Alix maintained loyally.

'Well, Danning seems to be doing it,' Gary pointed out reasonably. 'Unleavened highbrow isn't the formula for success.'

The phone rang and Gary reached for it. 'Pearson,' he said briskly. 'Oh, hi, Val!' He looked at Alix and winked. 'No, she's not here at the moment, Val.'

Alix pointed to herself and Gary put up his hand and shook his head. 'Well, I'd say she was the obvious choice, wouldn't you? You *wouldn't.*' He gave Alix a swift glance. 'On the contrary, Val, I think you've got a lot to be thankful for. Really? I'm staggered . . . .

Who's *they*?' he asked sharply. 'Sure, I like her. She's a good kid. . . . I can't stand it when you're bitchy, Val. . . . If you're feeling so dissatisfied why don't you have a talk to him yourself? Oh, what a jungle world we live in . . . you've told me all that before. . . . You *can* do your job, I'm not denying it for a minute. Well, I can't talk now, Val. It seems to be you've got yourself bogged down in some good old-fashioned jealousy. . . . *Ouch*!'

'Did she hang up on you?' Alix leaned over and patted his shoulder.

'I don't know anybody who can slam the phone down like Val,' Gary reflected. 'She's madder than a hornet about all the assignments Danning's been giving you.'

'I don't think he treats us very differently,' said Alix. 'She got the trip to Fiji to cover all the fashion shots.'

'And you got to interview Lewis Wollcott, Raylene Webb and a visiting American film star. It put her nose out of joint.'

'It gets harder and harder to please Val,' Alix murmured wryly, and launched herself out of her chair. 'If anyone wants me, I'm going down to Records.'

For the rest of the afternoon she spent her time reading up everything she could on Richard Kaufmann. She learned that he was born in Germany and brought to Australia by his parents at the age of two. Both his parents were professional musicians, so it came as no surprise when their son inherited their combined abilities and then some. At the age of twelve, established as a child prodigy, he was sent to the famous Juilliard School in New York City to continue his studies. The money was raised by the people of his own town, who continued to support him right up until the time of his debut. At twenty-two he won an international piano competition which established him in his career. He was twice married, first to an American socialite who was tragically killed in a plane crash a few years later, then to the Italian-born, Metropolitan-based diva Adriana Crespi. The marriage had broken up after a tempestuous twelve months.

Scarcely time for a honeymoon, Alix considered, and slammed the heavy files back into place. Public people had no private lives at all, so it seemed only fair he photographed so beautifully. She turned around and looked down at Adriana Crespi's pictured face. She was a magnificent-looking woman; on the grand scale and surely years older than Kaufmann? She peered closer then thought she had better look up Adriana Crespi. Not that divas ever gave within a decade of their correct age.

Her back was turned to the door when Valerie Turner walked in, her nose crinkled with distaste at the whispers of dust.

'What are you doing down here?' she asked without ceremony.

'Oh, hi, Val!' Alix swung around with the offhand greeting. 'Just a little research.'

'Why don't you give it to me straight?' Val challenged a little bitterly. 'He's given you another assignment.'

'Well, he's given me one ever since he arrived,' Alix returned reasonably. 'I mean, that's my job, isn't it, Val?'

'I suppose you think I'm bitchy?'

'I never thought to apply such a word!' Alix lied.

'Well, I don't think it's fair.' Val turned the open file her way. 'Adriana Crespi,' she muttered, her eyes narrowing, 'what do you know about that?' She sat down very slowly and carefully in a chair. 'It's Kaufmann, isn't it?'

With anyone else it wouldn't have mattered, but Alix didn't want the other girl to know. Val would sell anyone down the river to get a story.

'It's *got* to be Kaufmann,' Val crowed, and looked up at Alix unsmilingly. 'How do you possibly think you can manage it?'

'I value my job.'

'And so far you've been very lucky,' Val exclaimed bitterly. 'I've got as much ability as you. I'd be able to interview Kaufmann just as well as you.'

'You're missing the point, Val,' Alix said quietly. 'I don't care if you do, only Danning gave it to me.'

'So I ask you why?' The older girl clenched her fist and gesticulated with it.

'Why don't you ask him?' Alix gave a tired smile and prepared to move off.

'That piece you did on Raylene Webb was corny. It lacked impact.'

'With respect, dear, Danning liked it.'

'You didn't write an honest line,' said Val, obviously smarting from that remark.

'Well, I couldn't really write that she's a pretentious little ass. What are you on about, Val, anyway? If you're dissatisfied with your assignments, go speak to Danning. Don't take it out on me. I only work here like everyone else.'

'Excuse me, dear,' Val interrupted, 'you've never worked a day in your life—your father a top architect, plenty of money. You couldn't have enjoyed it when your fiancé chucked you.'

'Oh, go away, you make me sick,' Alix sighed, and it was pretty near the truth.

'All right, I will.' Val got her hand on the door, her face so distorted with anger, the freckles that matched her tawny hair stood out on her matt white skin. 'The question of talent doesn't even arise around here lately. For some reason Carl is showing you a marked preference, and I promise you that's going to change.'

'Good. I'll be glad of a little competition.'

'Wouldn't you just!' Val muttered, completely losing her sometime mask of good fellowship. 'No one looking at you would realise you're as pushy as you are. This is the third assignment you've stolen from me. I just know I could write a terrific article on Kaufmann, not waste my time searching through dreary files.'

'Then you're very welcome,' Alix sighed. 'Go and tell Danning what you've decided.'

It was exactly what Val needed to go up in flames. With the full knowledge of what she was doing, because they all knew the lock was faulty, she got hold of the outer door and slammed it hard behind her.

'So there, you silly bitch!' Alix sank back in the chair with a moaning breath. What a nasty world it was, to be sure. Now she would have to ring Gary and ask him to bail her out. She reached out a hand and picked up the phone. Drat Val and her childish tricks!

Gary answered, almost breathless. 'Pearson.'

'Get down here right away,' said Alix in a suspenseful voice.

'Darling, look, I'm sorry!' Gary shouted at her. 'But I have to fly. Tell me another time. Tomorrow. I'll be all ears.'

'*Gary*!' Alix cried, but he had already put down the receiver.

'Oh, damn!' In a bit of a panic she glanced at the electric clock to the left of the door. It was almost five. She just couldn't sit there and hope for a miracle. No one came down to the basement at that time of day. She rang Val's extension and Val herself picked up the phone.

'Are you ready to let me out?' Alix asked more politely than she felt. In many ways Val was a strange girl, with a sadistic bent of mind.

'Who *is* this?' Val asked, though she had long since committed the younger girl's tones to memory.

'A fellow worker who has to get home to cook the dinner.'

'Wonderful. How wonderful!' Val sneered. 'You're a very devoted sister.'

'All right, Val,' Alix returned evenly, 'the game's over. Let me out.'

'Go to hell! You won't die.'

Val crashed down the phone and Alix shut her eyes. She was continually being suprised by Val's feline spite.

'Have faith!' she muttered to herself, and rang another couple of extensions.

Naturally everyone had made a bolt for the door. She stood up, smoothed her hair as though to calm her mind, then sat down again. She *had* to ring through to Danning, because he, by God, wasn't a clock-watcher.

'Danning.'

His voice surprised her, it was so darned attractive.

'It's Alix Conroy here,' she said, trying to sound cool.

'I know that, Conroy.'

The instant sarcasm didn't make her feel good. For an instant she would have liked to borrow Val's phone-slamming technique, but it would have been a challenge he would have picked up with glee.

'That's all right, Conroy, if you've only rung to say hello. I'm sure it doesn't count that I'm busy.'

Alix decided she had better speak up immediately. 'Will you come down and let me out,' she said bluntly. 'I'm in the basement.'

'*I* see,' he said, sounding so condescendingly male she could have screamed. 'I take it you've locked yourself in.'

'It's not in the least amusing!'

'Can you manage there for a little while?' he said. 'I have to make a phone call.'

He did it deliberately. Of course he did. She shuddered with exasperation, then started to laugh, realising he was having his bit of fun.

He must have decided to make his phone call later, for in under a minute he had the door open, ramming a stopper underneath it.

'If you'll just step this way, Miss Conroy.'

'Thank you.' She stood up and came around the desk. 'You've got to promise me you'll get this door fixed.'

'Yes, ma'am.' He put his hand on the lock, trying it. 'Are you ready to go home?'

'I am.'

'Then I'll give you a lift.'

How did *he* know her car was being serviced? She stopped and glanced back over her shoulder. 'It's quite all right. I'll manage on the bus.'

Their eyes locked for a moment, his with the familiar glint, and she bit her lip.

'I've a question for you, Conroy.'

'Fire away.'

'Why do you dislike me so much?'

It's easy, she thought, still pinned by that warring glance. 'To be sure, I admire you enormously,' she said coolly, pressing her luck.

'Wouldn't it be comical if we both got locked in until the morning?'

For some reason, and she fumed and fussed about it later, Alix blushed. There was something about Carl Danning that frightened her. The powerful, male virility, she thought, repelled her. It would be a shocking, threatening experience to be locked in anywhere with Danning, with no will or energy left to fight him.

'Do you know how you're looking at me?' he asked a little tautly.

'I'm sorry.' She had to blink her grey eyes to break contact. 'I suppose I'm a little shaken.'

'I'm not a savage, Conroy,' he said gently. 'And I don't like being thought one. Or treated like one either.'

'I assure you I don't think of you in that light.' But I *do*. She forced herself to move at normal speed to the stairs. Look at how harshly he had treated silly little Sally.

'Then you'll allow me to drive you home?'

He was coming up the stairs after her and their

fingers accidentally brushed on the rail.

She had to swallow over the shock waves that jolted through her body, angered and confused by his easy power over women. Including *her*. She wasn't immune, the fact shamed her. 'Fine.' She tried for a normal tone, but it came out cool and brittle. 'Peter will be expecting me.'

They were gliding away from the car park before she could contribute another word. And even then she only mentioned the name of her suburb.

'Relax, Jumpy,' Carl Danning said tightly. 'I know where you live.' His coal-black eyes swept her profile, every line of his own dark, formidable face tense. 'Tell me about this brother of yours.'

'Don't think he's pampered,' Alix began a little heatedly. God, it was impossible, they were both so mutually antagonistic.

'Did I say that?' He accelerated and the Jaguar leapt forward to overtake a small Honda being driven by an extremely nervous lady driver.

Probably she had seen him coming up in her rear vision, Alix thought. *That* car and *that* face behind the wheel. It would make any nervous woman go tense with dread.

'Peter's fourteen,' she said, pulling her tattered nerves together. 'He's really very clever. He wants to be an architect.'

He nodded and said with what seemed to be genuine warmth, 'Like his father.'

'It means a great deal to us both,' said Alix.

'And you really believe in him, don't you?'

'I do.' Alix's lovely mouth smiled and her grey eyes shimmered with love. 'He's going to be brilliant and he's a very good boy. It's not easy for anyone to be orphaned and very hard on a young boy. Peter is coping very well. He's special.'

'It sounds to me like he's got a special kind of sister. How do you intend to raise the money to send him on to university?'

'There'll be enough,' she said, and felt the raw edge of devastation. 'I was able to put away a lot of what we got on the house.' And how they both longed for it. Her father's work. All that wonderful, calm authority.

'I hear it's going to be on the market again,' he told her, and shot her a hard, assessing glance.

'*What?*' She spun her head in shock.

'I was speaking to McNeill the other day. He's been offered a big job in the States. His wife's none too happy, but I'm sure he'll be able to convince her. Not too many people would pass up that kind of money.'

'I'm simply stunned.' She looked at him suspiciously. 'Are you sure?'

'I'm sure.' He glanced at her sideways. 'What's upset you anyway?'

'We hated leaving our home,' she said passionately. 'It seemed as if it was all we had left of our father, our old life. At least the McNeills appeared to love it as much as we did. I don't want any more people in the house.'

'Aren't you being a tiny bit unrealistic?' He slowed as he came to the curve that led up Alix's block of home units. 'It's not your house any more.'

'I don't need you to tell me,' she shook her head. 'Obviously you have no attachment to property.'

'Sure you don't want to hear the story of my life?' his mouth twisted ironically.

'You've got other reporters,' she said shortly, proof that she wasn't herself. He could sack her.

He whistled softly through his teeth. 'I hope that's because you're just plain scared.'

'Of what?' She sounded defensive, even to herself.

'Of our spending more than a few minutes alone together.'

He drew over to the kerb and the instant the car stopped Alix opened up the door. 'Thank you, Chief.'

'Hold it.' He leant over the console and looked up at her. 'I ain't finished yet.'

'No?' She lifted her delicate dark brows. The princess to the peasant.

'I'm having a few people over Saturday night.'

'I'm going to the ballet myself,' she told him sweetly with no hesitation.

'I don't think you understand me,' his black eyes blazed into life. 'I need *you* to act hostess. Business more than pleasure. One of our guests is Senator Boyle—I take it you *have* heard of him?'

'Surely you don't want me to interview him?' The Senator was a bachelor and known to be a ladies' man.

'Saunders can do that. You can keep him happy just sitting beside him at the table. I'm protecting our interest.'

'I really am going to the ballet,' she said.

'There are plenty of other nights.' Deliberately he switched on the radio, even if he kept the volume low. 'I'm wasting my time here. I've got work to do. See you Saturday, Conroy. I'm going to leave everything up to you—the dinner menu, flowers, the works.'

'For heaven's sake, *why*?' She was doing her best to understand. 'There are plenty of women, you know.'

'Ah yes,' his insolent eyes narrowed over her, 'but they haven't got your class. Just tell me when you want to look over my apartment and I'll lend you a key.'

'Put it this way,' she had to dip her blonde head just to see him, 'why don't you engage professional caterers? Any good-looking, fairly intelligent woman would keep the Senator happy.'

'Not *too* intelligent,' he said sarcastically. 'Politicians as a rule don't like being questioned. On the other hand, men really do prefer blondes.'

'Whatever you say, Mr Danning.' Hauteur came easily to her, her response to the way he needled her. 'Thank you for the lift.'

'I don't think you mean to thank me at all, but never mind.' He lifted his hand in a mock salute. 'Don't go to a lot of trouble on Saturday. But I want things *just right*!'

Alix moved her head a little fretfully, feeling a headache starting behind her eyes. 'This is terribly short notice.'

'I'm sure you'll cope. There'll be no more than twelve of us—any more would defeat the whole purpose. See me in the morning. I don't care how much you spend.'

She shut the door a little violently, or so she thought, but it was so heavy compared with her own car it didn't shut properly and she had to try again.

If Carl Danning caught the hint of temper he gave no sign of it. Anyway, with the air-conditioning, the

windows were all up. Alix lifted her hand in a hypo-
critical gesture of farewell, then turned determinedly
away. Drat Danning! She could feel the adrenalin
pumping in her; the anger, hostility, excitement.
How could he possibly appreciate *her* help? Not that
she was going to be intimidated by the thought of
arranging a dinner party for twelve. Providing he
gave her a free hand. Her mother had been a superb
hostess, a beautiful, stylish woman with a great sense
of quality. They had entertained on a lavish scale in
the old days, combining business with pleasure. Both
her parents had liked nothing better than to have
friends over and they lived up to the hilt of a leading
architect's income.

Alive, her father would have gone on making wonderful money and his children would have grown up
secure, but in her final year at university, Alix's
parents had been killed in a spectacular highway
collision. Six vehicles had been involved, four innocent people including a child had been killed and a
young man arrested and convicted on a dangerous
driving charge. That was two years ago, and every
time Alix heard a car's brakes squeal shrilly she bit
her lip in pain. Sudden, unbearable pain, though the
first agony was over. She had to be strong, for Peter's
sake. Whenever the going got tough, that was always
her thought. Peter's loss had been greater than her
own. Her childhood had been wonderfully happy and
secure. She had been blessed almost up to the age of
twenty-one, but Peter had been introduced to grief
too early. It was her job to make it up to him.

As soon as Peter heard his sister's key in the lock he
rushed out to greet her.

'Hi!' He put his arm around her and hugged her. They were very close—now, more than ever. 'Anything special happen today?'

'Enough for me!' Alix smiled at him and together they walked back into the kitchen where Peter's homework was spread all over the table.

'So are you going to tell me?' he demanded.

'First of all, what do you want for tea?'

'A lot, I'm hungry.'

'You're always hungry,' grinned Alix. 'You must have hollow legs.' She was tall herself for a girl, but Peter was already over her head. A handsome boy, very much like their father to look at, blessed with a sunny nature and a seemingly inexhaustible energy. 'Steak do and salad?'

'Sure, Mom.' Sometimes he forgot and it came out just like that. He was still frowning at a technical drawing and she was sure he hadn't even noticed, but she had to turn away very quickly. 'I meant to buy an apple pie, but I didn't have time. The boss drove me home.'

'You don't really like him, do you?' Peter suddenly lifted his blue eyes.

'No matter how I try.' She lifted the salad ingredients out of the crisper.

'Don't make it too obvious,' he said. 'It would be terrible to lose your job.'

'I don't think I'm going to do that.' Peter was very adult in his perceptions. 'As a matter of fact, he's given me a new assignment and I'm to host a dinner party for him Saturday night.'

'Hostess, don't you mean?'

'Oh, well—' Alix shrugged and tied an apron

around her waist. 'You don't find it unusual?'

'Do you?' Peter was giving her his full attention. 'He's not interested in you, is he?'

'Sometimes he has trouble just being civil.'

'That's nothing,' Peter considered from his wealth of experience. 'All things have meaning. The way people react. There's this girl on the bus, scowls at me every afternoon, but I have it from a high authority she thinks I'm real cool.'

'Surely not!' Alix laughed.

'The only trouble is, she's dumpy, but she's got a pretty face. Even when she's treating me like the enemy.'

'So what you're saying is, nothing is unplanned?' Alix's grey eyes turned speculative.

'Well, I mean, he wants to get socially involved.'

'Maybe he's heard I'm a good cook.'

'Don't think it's not important,' said Peter. 'It makes sense for a girl to learn how to cook properly. A terrible cook could damage a marriage and then a guy would have to return home.'

'I don't know that guys think about that beforehand,' Alix patted him kindly. 'But don't worry, I'll make all your serious girl-friends cook us a full dinner.'

'Spoken wisely.' Peter frowned and began to put his books together. 'I've got to take this into my room. I've got a ton of work to get through.'

'I'll call you,' said Alix.

Peter half-smiled and moved off. 'Remember, style is all, and you've got it. I'd watch that Danning character if I were you.'

CHAPTER TWO

WHEN Alix arrived at the office next morning, Gary was softly cursing to himself over a phone call.

'Hi, darling,' he broke off to look up at Alix and smile. 'The only good thing about today is waiting for you to come in.'

'What a line!'

'It's the truth, then.' Gary rocked back in his chair and sighed. 'I've had almost three hours' sleep.'

'The baby?'

'Our own little darling!' Gary yawned. 'All our other kids were so cheerful, but this one is a little monster.'

Alix clicked her tongue soothingly. 'Would you like me to get you a cup of coffee?'

'*Love* one!' Gary crooned. 'I didn't take breakfast this morning. Marj and I had a fight.'

'Poor old Marj!' Alix gave him a friendly smile. 'I suppose you didn't try to stop her getting up to the baby?'

'She seldom allows me,' Gary sniffed. 'It was very different last night. If she carries on like this, I'll leave her.'

'Never.' Alix walked to the coffee dispenser and poured out two coffees. 'Where would you get another marvel like Marj? Pretty and friendly, an excellent mother, a good wife.'

'I can't abide her when she's snaky.' Gary sipped at

the terrible coffee appreciatively. 'The truth is, Alix, though a man can live with the same woman for a long time, he can never hope to understand her.'

'You don't much like a woman's mystery?' Alix pulled the phone book towards her.

'By the way,' Gary jerked straight suddenly, 'what was it you wanted to see me about yesterday?'

'Promise to keep it confidential?'

'You know me.' Gary placed his hand on his heart.

'Dear old Val locked me in the basement.'

'Deliberately?' Gary emphasized the word to show that although he had asked the question he wasn't in any doubt.

Alix nodded. 'We all know the lock. I even rang her later and asked her to let me out, but she told me to drop dead. Or words to that effect.'

'Insensitive girl!' Gary's round blue eyes crinkled with laughter. 'Maybe she was born with the moon rising in Scorpio!'

'Or the sun in Sagittarius?'

'I don't believe in the stars, do you?' Gary finished off his coffee and put the carton through the disposal slot. 'For a start, they promised me romance this week, and I got the distinct impression I'd be locked out tonight.'

'Maybe you should look around for a little gift in the lunch hour.' Alix ran her finer down the Kaufmanns in the phone book. There were only six, four with a double n and none with the initial R. She hadn't really expected to find his number listed. He was a very private man. And how!

'I suppose it's impossible to get a silent number from Telecom?' she asked.

Gary didn't even hesitate. 'Impossible, dear. Who is it you're wanting to call?'

'Richard Kaufmann.' Alix slammed the book shut.

Gary whistled. 'Now I really would expect poor old Val to get mad!'

'I guess he thinks I can handle it.'

'And you can!' Gary patted her with a sympathetic hand. 'But don't think it's going to endear you to Val.'

'She's a good journalist,' Alix pointed out.

'The trouble is, dear, she hasn't got a very even temper.'

'I'm a bit concerned about Kaufmann's right to privacy,' Alix said seriously.

'But he's *our* Richard Kaufmann!' Gary opened his eyes wide again. Humorous eyes even when romance wasn't going his way. 'Think of it that way. He's almost public property. Surely I recall his home town sponsored him for years?'

'They did. I read up everything I could on him.' Alix rested her chin on her hands. 'How do I get to him? I can't ring him on the phone.'

'He must go out to the supermarket.' Gary put a new cartridge into his typewriter. 'Waylay him there. Aren't you Billy Blinkhorn? That kind of thing. What a surprise meeting *you*. Drop a couple of cans on his toe—he's injured, you've got him where you want him. It's all yours.'

'He's fortunate, of course, very fortunate, that I've had nursing experience.'

'And your interests are mixed.' Gary warmed to it. 'You have all his records—six hundred and fifty-four. All grouped. Albeniz to What's-'is-name.'

'It's a super idea,' said Alix, 'but it says here, he has a Chinese manservant.'

'So should every man worth his salt.'

'*Please*, Gary,' Alix sighed. 'How am I going to get to him? The manservant will do the shopping.'

'Let me think.' Gary hit his forehead. 'What about a private detective? Or a hidden newsreel camera. You could dress up in a white uniform and go fix his phone. You could even, come to that, simply knock on his door. You're a collector of Oriental antiques.'

'I think I'd be told to leave.'

'In addition to which, you speak fluent Chinese. The manservant offers to help. It's likely he's got some relatives behind the Bamboo Curtain, and your future husband may just be able to help. He's in the Ministry. Neglect to tell him which one.'

'I suppose I could just knock on the door,' Alix murmured, ignoring Gary's rambling.

'Say your foot hurts. You've ricked your ankle—worse.'

'After all, I could wrench my ankle and have to sit down for a while,' Alix mused.

'It will be a damned sight worse after you pull yourself up all those stairs,' Gary told her. 'Unless he's shifted in the last few months he has a penthouse apartment over on the North Shore.'

'What suburb?' Alix's smoke-coloured eyes lit up.

'It's a big city, girl. The question is, could you play a cleaning lady?'

'A Sadie, that sort of thing?'

'It's a little jewel of a role. Otherwise I won't be able to get you inside.'

'You know something you're not saying?' Alix

turned in her chair to look at him wonderingly.

'It could be totally immoral, unethical, whatever.'

'*Gary!*'

He sat away from the typewriter and spread his hands. 'You know, since the baby, Marj has a cleaning lady in to help her?'

'You don't tell me everything.'

'All the same, she has. I'm what's known as an indulgent husband, kind, considerate, caring. Marj needs help, she gets it. It is not, as some men would say, wasting money. . . .'

'*Tell* me!' Alix heaved herself out of her chair with the faint notion of shaking Gary.

'I'm fairly sure—not one hundred per cent, mind—our cleaning lady was sent around to the Kaufmann place. She was proud of it. Marj told me a little time later. She was proud of it too. *Her* cleaning lady cleaning for Richard Kaufmann—that put us in the big league. Of course, it could have been our cleaning lady's best friend. Anyway, I'm certain it was the same firm.'

Alix held his blue eyes. 'Are you suggesting I do something shameful like bribe a Sadie?'

'Something like that, yes,' Gary nodded his head.

She stared at him. 'It's not as though they'd ever *do* it. After all, they would have to abandon the idea of ever going back again. He'd be furious at such an underhand trick.'

'So tell him the whole distressing story,' Gary urged her. 'You've tied up the regular Sadie and left her in the broom closet. You've got your story and our cleaning lady has still got her job.'

'It's shameful,' said Alix. 'How would I even know he was in?'

'Watch the building,' Gary suggested. 'Or be prepared to pay someone else to do it. I've heard he drinks heavily.'

'Not a pianist!' Alix shook her head.

'Maybe he doesn't play so good these days.'

'I can't do it, Gary,' she wailed. 'It's dishonest and it's looking for trouble.'

'I'll check with Marj tonight,' Gary promised. 'It will give us something to talk about.'

The office boy came through a side door calling cheerfully: 'The photographs ready, Mr Pearson? Hello, Miss Conroy.' Cheeky brown eyes went to Alix and stayed there. 'Haven't got your car back yet, I see. Maybe I could drive you home.'

'*You?*' Gary exclaimed, and slapped a batch of photographs into the boy's hand. '*You*, boy? Have you even been permitted to take out a licence?'

'More. I passed on my first test.' This, very breezily.

'The examiner too much of a coward to come back the second time?' Gary snorted, and waved his hand dismissively. 'Remember, boy, you come to this office for business. Pleasure, no.'

'Still want me to get your lunch?' the office boy grinned, and walked off unperturbed.

'I do—and don't forget you have to account for every penny.' The door swung shut and Gary shook his fair, balding head. 'I don't know what the younger generation is coming to? Trying to chat you up!'

'Cheek, I grant you.' Alix agreed vaguely. She was still looking at a file of newspaper clippings, the top story headed by a photograph of Richard Kaufmann.

It said that the internationally acclaimed concert pianist had come home for a much needed and deserved rest.

'Good-looking bloke!' Gary said enviously. He stood up and glanced over Alix's shoulder. 'Plenty of *hair*.' Though he was only thirty-five, Gary's crown was like a skating rink. 'If you ask me, you won't have any trouble at all. Most men would relish being tricked by a beautiful girl. Look at James Bond.' He picked up another clipping and sighed voluptuously. 'I *dream* about women like this.'

'Adriana?' Alix burst out laughing. 'She's some dish!'

'Opera singers are supposed to be built. You know that.'

Bill Baume, one of the photographers, came to the door and called: 'Can I see you for a moment, Gary?'

'Sure.' He put the clipping down and said to Alix over his shoulder, 'I'll have to study those some more.'

Left alone, Alix leant over her typewriter feeling uncertain, frustrated. How did one, short of trickery, get an interview from a man who was notorious for his inaccessibility? As she couldn't reach him by phone should she formally request an interview in writing? A sheer waste of time. All the magazines went after interviews with famous people, usually photographed in their own home, but it was common knowledge that Richard Kaufmann had refused every single request from the top journalists and the stars of the television shows. In almost a year no one had coaxed a word out of him, let alone a party piece. He had obviously gone into a serious decline.

And Gary's idea? She wasn't at all happy about

that. Of course it could just work, but it seemed kind of sneaky. Journalists often had to use all their wiles to get a story, but she wasn't too enthusiastic about pretending to be a cleaning lady. Not that she couldn't pass inspection. A coloured uniform would do it; maybe a scarf over her head. Her hair was fairly eye-catching.

'*Conroy!*'

The tone was just barely tolerant and Alix swung around to see Carl Danning staring at her with a mocking, faintly weary expression.

'If you've got to struggle to stay awake, maybe you'd better get yourself a cup of coffee.'

'Actually,' she returned briskly, 'I was working on a modus operandi.'

'Really?' he smiled sarcastically. 'I thought you were being just plain rotten lazy. If you come into my office, we can talk.'

'So here we are,' she said, after he had waved her into a chair.

'Here's the guest list.' He passed a sheet of paper over to her. 'Know any of them?'

'To be sure, from reputation.'

'Does that mean some of them don't make the grade?'

'I can't think what you mean?' she looked back at him clear-eyed and innocent.

'Your tone implied that at least one of them didn't come from your own social background.'

'Ah, but then he's coming up on the scale,' she said fearlessly. 'How gracious of you to ask him.'

'He's about to become one of the top entertainers in the country.'

'I think he's woeful myself.'

'Try not to let it make any difference. Anyway, he's very kindly consented to come.'

'I hope you asked him to leave his guitar at home.'

'Enjoy yourself, Conroy,' he said snappily.

'Shall we discuss the menu?' she asked.

'I couldn't stand to.'

'What about dress?'

'Something suitable for your patrician blood.' He leaned back a little and opened the centre drawer of his desk. 'I'm sure we're going to enjoy ourselves enormously.'

'But you won't tell me what you want?' she said, for the first time, rather helplessly.

'Girls like you are supposed to know. Notice what an interesting group you have to work with—a politician, a pop star, the head of a big organisation, a couple from the media. . . .'

'You did say you want the best?'

'My dear, I've been enjoying the best for a long time now,' he assured her, his dark face sardonic. 'Here's the key to my apartment. I don't think you'll be ashamed of it.'

Alix ignored the implications behind his remarks. 'I'll try to get out there today.'

'How energetic!' His black eyes narrowed over her. 'You seem to know where I live.'

'I do.' She answered casually. 'Gary happened to mention that you had the penthouse at Bentleigh. If it's all right with you, I'll have Maggie Connolly in to do the catering. She's a superb cook and her girls are very neat and efficient. It's perhaps needless to point out that she's quite expensive.'

'Did you say something?' he asked blandly.

'All right, then,' she stood up briskly and dangled the key. 'I promise I won't lose this.'

'It's best to know what you're getting into.' He leant back idly, his eyes sliding over her.

Put *that* way, Alix couldn't find an answer. There was something in the way he always looked at her that provoked a severe reaction. Mostly the heat of anger.

'You haven't mentioned your plan about Kaufmann?' said Carl Danning at the moment she was reaching for the door.

'I'm working on it.' She looked very slender and graceful in a classic style white linen skirt and a gold-toned tailored silky shirt. One of the favoured few, and not a working girl at all.

'The easy answer,' he said dryly. 'I imagine you've found out he has an unlisted number?'

'I was thinking of calling to the door.'

'You're free to handle it any way you like.' He put his hand out to the phone and held it. 'If you don't know where he lives, I'll tell you. Norfolk Towers over on the Shore.'

'Why, thank you.' She stared back at him in surprise.

'It's going to be hard enough, so I thought I'd give you a head start. I believe too, from my sources, he never emerges from his bomb shelter until at least eleven o'clock in the morning.'

'He probably has a lot of late nights,' she said flippantly.

'Also, if you're really keen, he jogs.'

'Like where?' Her grey eyes lit to silver.

'I'm giving you a powerful lot of help,' he muttered, and began to dial his number. 'The park across the street. If you want to join him, and it shouldn't be too difficult, try getting there around dusk.'

'I could be mugged,' she pointed out.

'No doubt. Get one of your boy-friends to tag along. Hello, Max? Danning,' he said into the receiver, and Alix closed the door. She was altogether happier about tackling Richard Kaufmann in the park. She didn't even need to buy jogging shoes. She had them.

The same afternoon, her routine jobs over, she took a run out to Bentleigh. It had been designed by a highly respected firm of architects and its units were all very pricey, but Alix had never liked it. It had no particular character, no innovative ideas, but because of its size and position a certain calm dignity. She wondered why Danning found its penthouse so desirable, but a minute after she let herself in, she knew.

Quite apart from a contemporary functionalism, it had the most fabulous view. Her breath caught in admiration and she crossed the beige-coloured carpet to find the catch on one of the floor-to-ceiling sliding glass panels.

Out on the sheltered terrace, lacy green trees stood in antique Chinese jardinières and there was a magnificent life-size Guy Boyd sculpture of a modern Venus, sensuous and serene. Alix touched it with a reverent hand, noting the recessed light spot that had been set into the eaves to shine on the sculpture. She would look beautiful lit up at night, as would the exquisite spangle of lights around the shore.

Carefully she shut the door again and locked it.

Not that anyone could get in that way, except maybe Spiderman. Everywhere throughout the huge open-plan living-dining room she found the most beautiful works of art; antique and modern, paintings, sculptures, screens, porcelain vases and pottery bowls. Cabinets hid the television and an elaborate sound system, and great pains had been taken with the lighting.

She ran her hand down a few switches, seeing how they washed the paintings and the various objects with light. It was very sophisticated and distinctive; the work of a genuinely creative man with an eye for fine things and the money to acquire them.

It rather jarred her. She preferred to think of Carl Danning as a vulgar upstart; it made things so much easier. A little resentfully she sat down in one of the neutral-toned sofas, imagining what her father might say about this room. He would like it; there was no question about that. He would even say to her one could tell a great deal about a person from their chosen environment. Carl Danning had come as a complete surprise to her, right from the beginning.

She sat there for a few moments reflecting on the man she worked for, then her mind came back to the task on hand. It was essential she get a clear picture of where everyone was to be seated. The fact that there were two dining settings had intrigued her immediately, now she saw that the dining tables resolved into one as the occasion demanded. No problem there.

She got up again and walked through to the kitchen. It was on the small side, but very cleverly designed; black and white and shiny and, as she might have expected, superbly practical. If Maggie wouldn't exactly relish its size, there was nothing about it that would put her in a temper. Probably he was a good cook as well, nothing would surprise her.

She had decided in advance she would confine her attention to the kitchen/dining areas—after all, that was all she was there for—but sheer feminine perversity more than curiosity drove her to look into the bedrooms. There were two; the guestroom, restful and harmonious, and the master bedroom that had considerably more drama about it. She had been hoping for a mirrored ceiling to fit his reputation, but that little detail was missing. Her forehead crinkled in concentration. Surely Sally had told her he had a mirrored ceiling in his bedroom. Indeed she had, and gurgled suggestively while she said it. If Sally hadn't exactly come right out and said it, she had hinted strongly at a shortlived but tempestuous affair. Maybe it was in some other place, though Gary had told her months ago that Danning had an apartment in Bentleigh.

What did she care anyway? She was being very vulgar herself, snooping where she wasn't supposed to be. At least the black quilted satin bedspread was a bit decadent, as well as the brilliant flash of Chinese red lacquer. He had been given a reputation and she intended he should stick with it.

The sound of a key being inserted in the front door nearly made her jump out of her skin. Surely he hadn't followed her out? The thought made her heart quiver in shock. The very last thing she wanted was to be left alone with him. She hurried out of the bedroom and along the corridor to the living room, mortified that she should be caught coming from that direction.

'Who's there?'

It was a woman's voice, sharp and a bit panicky.

'Alix Conroy.' Alix hastened to identify herself. 'I'm from the office.'

The woman who stood in the entrance hall was annoyed and showed it. 'I assume you have some form of identification?'

'Yes,' Alix agreed, and made no move to get it. Instead she said: 'I've been asked to check on a few things for Mr Danning.'

'Such as?' The woman was still staring frozen-faced, but her voice was quite vehement.

'He's having a dinner party on Saturday night,' Alix returned coolly, realising that as the woman had a key she was either a relative or a very close friend.

'I realise that. What exactly has it to do with you?'

'I'm organising it,' said Alix, and picked up her handbag.

'You're what?' the woman exclaimed incredulously. 'This is too fantastic!'

'May I ask your name?' Alix asked mildly.

The brunette ignored her. 'Stay there, if you don't mind. I'm going to ring Carl.'

'Certainly, if you want to.' Alix answered with exaggerated politeness and sat down again on the sofa. If looks could kill, she was already dead.

The woman walked back to the entrance hall and deliberately faced Alix.

Keeping her eye on me, Alix thought. How odd! She felt her nerves tauten in resentment. Though the woman had Danning's colouring, dark hair and dark eyes, she was certain they were no relation, unless sisters suffered from an unwholesome jealousy. But she *was* very good-looking. Thirtyish and ultra-elegant. Probably heavy dieting contributed towards making her so mean-minded.

'Mr Danning.' She was frowning down at the ground. 'Yes, you may.' The tone conveyed, what a nerve! 'Barbra Gould.'

Of course! Barbra Gould of Gould Interiors. Which didn't explain why she was acting so thoroughly suspicious and angry.

'Carl?' The curt tone underwent a remarkable sea change. 'Barbra.'

So it was like that, was it? Alix thought, disgusted.

'There's a young woman here who claims to come from your office. She's sitting right here on the sofa.'

'No, she's not!' Alix exclaimed dryly. 'She's walking to the door.'

'Put her on?' The fruity tone faltered. 'Then you *did* send her?'

'I believe I told you that,' said Alix.

'But really, darling, you know you can ask me *anything*!' It was very nearly a wail. 'I'm never *that* busy . . . very well.' Barbra held out the receiver to Alix, apologising rather stiffly. 'I hope I didn't offend you, but I had to be sure.'

'Alix Conroy,' Alix said shortly into the phone.

'Evidently you made a bad impression on Barbra?'

'I saw that at once.'

Barbra Gould was now sitting back in an armchair looking very much at home.

'Don't feel too badly,' Carl Danning said dryly. 'What did you make of the place?'

'Naturally, if it was done by Gould Interiors. . . .'

'The hell it was!' he interrupted bluntly. 'The dining tables come together.'

'I realised that. Probably I would like to shift them around.' She was thinking of the night-time view.

'Yes, I move them around a good bit. Anything else?'

'Sure you wouldn't like to change your mind?'

'You mean Barbra?'

'It seems a terribly good idea,' she said satirically.

'I'm not in the habit of mixing business with pleasure,' he said.

She had to shut her ears to such lies. 'Shall I put Miss Gould back on?'

'It's *Miz* Gould, acutally,' he told her. 'She did have one modern marriage, but it broke up.'

'God knows why!' Alix said sarcastically. She put the receiver down gently on the table and called out, 'Mrs Gould, Mr Danning would like to speak to you. I have to get back to the office.'

Barbra Gould got up immediately, smoothing her skirt over her hard, trim hips. 'Carl could so easily have asked me. I would never say no.'

'Why not ask him now?' Alix suggested. After all, *she* didn't want to go to his rotten party.

When she got back to the office, Danning took her to task.

'Would you kindly not interfere in the arrangements I've made,' he said testily.

'Sorry, I thought I was helping.'

'How was that?' He raised his black eyes.

'She's a very stylish lady,' said Alix, sustaining his gaze with some effort.

'Are you looking for a way out?'

'No, of course not. I'll be on duty on Saturday night.' She darted to the door and got her hand on the knob. It was amazing how he always seemed to change her breathing. 'I think I'll get masses of white carnations.'

'*Ciao*, Conroy,' he said without lifting his head. 'Be a very good girl and go!'

'Danning has come up with a great idea,' Alix told Gary, when she got back to her desk. 'It seems my quarry jogs.'

'Stupendous!' Gary ripped a sheet out of the type-writer, screwed it up and threw it in the waste paper basket. 'How did he discover that?'

'I didn't ask.' Alix began to collect her things. 'If anyone asks, I've gone off in hot pursuit of a story.'

'You've only got to flash those gorgeous legs.'

'Actually,' she said, 'I intend to work up to it. Make a friend of him first. A casual wave every evening.'

'I hope it's a decent area,' said Gary, and gave a disapproving frown. 'The world seems to be full of rapists these days.'

'Now why tell me a thing like that?' she patted him on the shoulder.

'Because you're a delightful girl and I've become very fond of you.'

'Don't worry,' she said encouragingly. 'I'll take care.'

CHAPTER THREE

THE park was almost empty when Alix arrived and it was another fifteen minutes before Richard Kaufmann emerged from the building opposite, cast a quick look from left to right, then jogged determinedly across the street.

'Bingo!' Alix clapped her hands together silently and gave a nervous laugh. He didn't look especially important or unapproachable in a T-shirt and shorts, nevertheless the lump in her throat was growing bigger all the time. Why was it he wouldn't give an interview in the normal way? It would make everything so much more dignified.

Quickly she got out of the car and locked it. At least there weren't any undesirables about. She had already checked the park out. This was an area of considerable tone and the local residents would be fiercely protective of this verdant little jewel on their doorstep. It was filled with beautiful shrubs and trees and, even now, birdsong. Probably Kaufmann had discovered peace on his private runs.

She slipped the car keys in the pocket of her cotton shirt and buttoned the flap down, starting off in the direction Kaufmann had taken. Such a world of intrigue she lived in, and public curiosity about celebrities was insatiable. An interview with Richard

Kaufmann just could be a sizzler, considering his looks, his talent and his somewhat legendary love life.

The path ahead was becoming very shadowy where the big trees met overhead. The thing to do would be to meet him coming the other way. Pardon me, Mr Kaufmann, but I've been sent by my magazine to waylay you. We thought it would be more fun in the park.

An elderly man with a red setter emerged from behind the first clump of shrubs and Alix nearly shrieked with fright.

'Ah, good evening,' the man said, just a tiny bit grumpy. He detested these joggers taking up the path.

Alix gave him a startled smile and kept on running. She had only been going a few seconds and already she was dead tired. It almost seemed despite her perfect slender figure that she was out of condition. She couldn't decently allow such a state of affairs to continue. Kaufmann had even done her a favour. She would talk to Peter about jogging in the morning, force him if she had to. Jogging wasn't exactly a pleasure, but there were important benefits, such as better reflexes. A boy on a bike had to slam on his brakes not to run into her.

'You should watch where you're going,' Alix called sharply.

'You don't own the place, lady.'

There was nothing worse than cheeky kids, Alix thought breathlessly, trying to bring some co-ordination to her arms and legs.

So preoccupied was she, she didn't see Richard Kaufmann go past her, and when she did catch his moving figure out of the corner of her eye, she could have slammed her head against a brick wall. He had been running like a professional when she was already dragging her feet. She wavered for a minute while she caught her breath, then she continued her run. After all, she had been considered very fleet of foot at school; a grey-eyed, long-legged blonde. It was a challenge, then, to do better.

A cooling breeze had blown up and it lifted the ribbon right out of her hair.

'Damn!' She couldn't even begin to rummage for it, it was growing too dark.

Kaufmann went past her again, a pale blur.

This was ridiculous. Any gentleman would have said hello. Once more around and she would have to give it away or run in the pitch dark. If she had been really resourceful she would have brought along a flashlight.

Distracted by all the odd little rustlings in the bushes, she ran faster than ever, pouring on the speed, with the result she went past Kaufmann like an Amazon. Her hair streamed out behind her, and now the park was dotted with evening spangles of light carrying her image to the wondering man. She looked splendid, like a goddess, all dazzling long legs and a silver mane. She should be holding aloft an Olympic flame.

Her heart bursting, Alix made it to the car. She couldn't remember when she had run like that, and Richard Kaufmann was definitely looking her way. How sweet! How heady! Tomorrow she would give him a little wave. Operations like this had to be dragged out in instalments. She inserted the key in the car door and turned it precisely. Kaufmann was still gazing her way, but it would be the greatest mistake to try to speak to him now. Much too easy. She hopped in like a girl who bore more than her fair share of social engagements and Kaufmann ran across the road with long strides, trembling with a desire to know the blonde goddess's name. Because he was a deeply sensitive man and a lover of beauty the sight of her running so poetically had lifted his downcast heart. Obsessed with his sacred privacy, he hadn't minded running with her at all.

By the time Alix arrived home she was exhausted.

'Dope!' grinned Peter, and further dishevelled her hair. 'You have to take it in stages.'

'I don't know, I thought it was easy!'

'Really?' Peter shrugged. 'Maybe it will be in a couple of weeks' time. Nothing to report?' He took the glass of water from her.

'It went well.' Alix managed a smile. 'In fact I'd say I set quite an example. There should be many more women jogging instead of indulging themselves with chocolate cake. Someone has to take the lead. When I last saw him he was looking at me with absolute approval.'

'But that doesn't mean anything,' said Peter. 'Wait until you show yourself in your true colours. It could be tragic to mislead an artistic type.'

'I could go straight up and tell him the whole story.'

'Tell him you're a worshipper of his art and you detest duplicity,'

'All of which is true.' Alix broke off as the telephone rang. 'Answer that, will you. I'm out of puff.'

'If you ask me, you'll be too stiff to run tomorrow,' Peter commented as he moved off.

Alix covered her face with her hands. She had better have a quick shower.

'It's for you, kid.' Peter came up behind her.

'Oh, damn,' Alix dragged herself up. 'Who is it?'

'Someone with a very classy voice. Very masterful and sexy.'

'Oh, *no!*' Alix looked at her brother in alarm. 'That sounds like Danning.'

'You mean he talks like that as well as everything else?'

Alix felt herself blush. 'Even when he's being really nasty. Go and beat me up a raw egg.'

'Or we'll get in a little exercise bike and you can pedal furiously.' Peter was finding it all vastly entertaining. While his sister went to answer the phone, he fell on the floor and started to do push-ups . . . six . . . seven . . . eight . . . he had always been energetic.

'Hello,' Alix said briskly into the phone.

'Congratulations,' Danning answered. 'I couldn't resist the temptation to ring up and tell you.'

'You don't mean you were there?'

'It's a lovely park.' His voice ranged from mockery to laughter. 'Frankly I think you reached him on half a dozen planes . . . aesthetic, athletic. . . . Precisely when are you going to speak to him?'

'It would have been too easy tonight,' she told him.

'I agree.'

The fact that he had been watching her disturbed her greatly. 'What I can't seem to grasp is, *why* you were there?'

'Because one of my staff members was involved. I felt protective,' he added dryly.

'I'm a thousand miles from believing it.'

'But then you're a very suspicious girl. One doesn't have to have white hair to feel paternal.'

'Anyway, it's a very safe and sober locale.' There had been a couple of cars about, but she would have noticed a Jag.

'My dear girl,' he said sardonically, 'evil is everywhere. I shall continue to keep an eye on you. A man with a mower . . . a gardener clipping off a dead head . . . even a jogger. I was one of the pioneers.'

'I didn't know you were so tenderhearted.' She didn't like it either. She had already made up her mind about him.

'In any case, it's interesting to know exactly how it turns out. I would say poor old Kaufmann is going to dream about you tonight. You looked incredibly fetching. For that matter, how do you feel?'

'Do you want the truth?'

'Not really. I have to go.'

Before she could get out another word, he had hung up.

'What a strange man!' Alix walked back into the living room muttering.

'What did he want?' Peter looked at her curiously. She had a lot of unaccustomed colour under her skin.

'Oh, to make some witty little remarks. It appears he went to the park to watch me.'

'Did he say why?'

'He was feeling protective.' Alix looked back at her brother dubiously.

'Where is this park anyway?' Peter asked, his smooth forehead crinkling in a frown.

'Oh, it's safe!' Alix assured him. 'I've never seen a more sedate area and it's very well lit.'

'Well then, why did Danning turn up? It seems a little strange to me. Are you sure you aren't his kind of woman?'

'Positive!' Alix put her hand to the small of her back and groaned. 'I met his type today.'

'Anyone special?'

'Ah, just another good-looking woman!' said Alix a little contemptuously.

'You've really got him cast as the heavy, haven't you?' Peter said absently, hunting up a reference book. 'I'd like to meet this guy.'

'Come and jog with me tomorrow night and we'll all get together. Now I'm going to have a shower, then I'll get dinner going.'

After all, she didn't have to run the following night, because it rained, but on Friday evening she set off determinedly. Peter hadn't come with her because she was allowing him to spend the weekend at his closest friend Rusty Maclean's place and so far she was certain she wasn't being tailed by Danning. When she had left the office he had still been in conference with Lester Palmer, the national advertising manager and Danning's own appointee. So much the better for *Impact*, Alix thought wryly. Lester was extremely good at his job and unquestionably Danning's man.

As she locked the car, she had the feeling that today was the day. It had been eventful so far, including another clash with Val, who managed to drop a cup of coffee over what she thought was Alix's work, but was really Gary's review of a major film. Both she and Gary had sat astounded, fascinated in their way by feline spite, for Val hadn't even said: 'Dear me!'

'She thinks she's going to get away with it,' Gary had said faintly, before gathering up his ruined work, 'but we'll see!'

'Try glueing her to her seat.' Alix had suggested before coming to Gary's aid.

Alix drove briskly around the park before it was closed to traffic. No hooligans, louts, larrikins, just in case Danning didn't show up. The same terrible kid on a yellow BMX, and as Alix drove past him, the ten-year-old said something through his clenched teeth. His own form of censorship, probably. There was a good dollop of delinquent in that child.

'*Paddy*!' someone called loudly from across the street, and to Alix's relief, the unholy Paddy got off and pushed his bike across the road.

'Coming, Mum!' he bellowed just as loudly.

Alix felt pleased with him, just the same. He had at least responded to his parent and he showed good road sense.

So much for a little practice! By the time she had made one circuit of the park, it was necessary for her to take a discreet breather. Maybe he was going to hibernate tonight. Plenty of people were going into the block of units, but no one was coming out. If Richard Kaufmann didn't turn up, she would be shattered. Her one flawless effort had been two nights ago. She couldn't possibly turn on that burst of speed twice.

Two elderly ladies leading balls of fluff waved greetings to each other and the man with the red setter Alix had noticed the other night stopped outside his front gate as though he couldn't make up his mind whether to brave the park or not. Nothing he liked better than to be alone, and his glance fell gloomily on the three women within immediate view.

'Oh, Major!' One of the women turned her head and waved her arm. 'Hurry up, lazy!'

Extraordinarily, the Major obeyed. Alix had to bend down and retie her shoelace to hide the smile on her face. When she straightened up, Richard Kaufmann was coming out of the building opposite.

The little dogs didn't let her go by without setting up a racket and the Major smirked at her sarcastically.

'Careless, don't you think?' one elderly lady asked her companions, 'running about at night.'

Alix didn't hear what the others thought. She was too far away. She couldn't stand her hair flying around her face, so tonight she had caught it back with an elastic band. No doubt it didn't look quite so attractive. He might not even recognise her.

On their first encounter, it seemed certain. He passed her with absolutely no reaction. Disappointment made her droop like a sunflower. This was all so embarrassing, ludicrous. She would probably get runner's knee for her efforts, and little else.

A big man walked across the grass and sat down on a park bench, an odious, hateful smile on his face.

Alix cast him a fierce, half defiant glare and increased her pace. He was *enjoying* this, the wretch! No doubt about it. He had even suggested this line of investigation. She heaved another deep breath and pulled her handkerchief out of her pocket, dabbing at her brow. He would enjoy seeing her make a perfect ass of herself, tearing round and round a green, deserted park.

The next time she passed Kaufmann again, she didn't even look at *him*, Carl Danning was too much on her mind. He was still sitting back on the bench, one arm thrown carelessly along the top rail, smiling a private, mocking smile. He wasn't worried about thieves, muggers, etc. He was *enjoying* himself. Light-hearted retaliation for the way she had treated him. Right from the beginning. The classic pay-back. Why hadn't she understood that earlier?

Everyone found it pretty hard to swallow, being made a fool of. Alix dropped her pace, distracted and discouraged, instinctively moving towards her car. The whole thing was downright undignified. It would be better to go and knock on Kaufmann's door, not let Carl Danning control her. She felt in her pocket for her keys and gave an audible little cry of dismay.

'Oh, no! No. No. *No!*' It was the last straw.

'May I help you?' A man's voice said behind her with real concern.

'Oh, yes, *please!*' She turned to him with an equally unfeigned reaction. 'I've lost my car keys.'

'The car is locked?' Richard Kaufmann drew alongside and peered in the car's gloomy interior.

'I'm afraid it is.' Alix jerked her head back a little wildly. 'They must be somewhere on the path. I had them in my pocket.'

'Keep calm,' Kaufmann advised her with a gentle sigh. 'We'll retrace your steps, shall we? Failing that, I could run you home. You must have a second lot of keys.'

'I do.' Alix drew a ragged breath, not fully in control of herself. How could she let him run her home when she lived on the other side of town? He would reach the obvious conclusion that she had set out to bewitch him, trap him, whatever. Even the most dedicated jogger found a venue closer home.

'You realise it will be difficult finding them?' he said.

'Thank you for helping me.' She gave him an honest luminous smile. 'I pulled my handkerchief out to dab my head and I must have lost them then. In which case we can pinpoint the spot, or at least a lot closer.'

With the famous pianist following closer at her heels, Alix broke into a little run. If the worst came to the worst, she could tell him a little story, say she was staying with a friend. Better, she could have him drop her off at Rusty's place. At least it was only a couple of miles away.

Down on their knees, they were facing each other.

'Look here, this is almost impossible at night,' he said firmly. 'I'll run you home so you can get your other key.'

'I couldn't ask it of you,' she murmured, burningly aware that Carl Danning was observing them from a distance off. 'If you could just let me use your phone?'

'It's no trouble, I assure you.' He stood up and took her hand, assisting her to her feet. 'Where do you live?'

'Sirius Street,' she said evasively. 'Please, just let me call.'

'As you wish.' He seemed to withdraw faintly, perhaps regretting the unaccustomed warmth of his offer. 'I live just across the street at the Towers. My name is Kaufmann, by the way.'

'Alix Conroy,' she told him, and decided in a split

second not to pretend she didn't recognise the name. 'Not *Richard* Kaufmann?'

'Well, yes.' He sounded more impatient than proud.

'I know your recordings well, Mr Kaufmann,' she said in a calm, unexcited voice. 'It must be marvellous to be so gifted.'

'Less marvellous than it once was.' They had reached the road and he took her elbow automatically.

'I expect one might feel like that with a demanding career.' She looked back for a second and saw Carl Danning salute her. More, she saw him dangling her car keys.

If he thinks he's going to throw me, he's got another think coming! Alix thought wrathfully. A car sped carelessly towards them and she clutched at Richard Kaufmann's arm, the very picture of femininity.

'What a fool!' Her voice, however, was crisp and annoyed. 'I don't know why all the stories about women drivers earn such good laughs. Men are by far the worst offenders.'

'Of course they are,' Richard Kaufmann agreed soothingly, when Carl Danning would undoubtedly have produced statistics and a dry laugh.

'Are you *sure* I'm not putting you to too much trouble? There must be a phone booth close by.'

'I'd be more than happy to drive you home, you know,' he said warmed again by her gesture. 'I have nothing else to do.'

Goodbye, story! Her mind was ticking over frantically. The only way out was to let him take her over to Rusty's place. It still didn't solve the problem of the key, but at least she wouldn't be breaking her cover.

'Well then, I can only say thank you.' I have no scruples at all, she thought. None. Maybe I never had them.

The smile he gave her in the foyer moved her to despair. It was so sweet and trusting. He was obviously a very nice man.

'I'm on the top floor,' he said, and pushed the button in the lift. 'It will only take me a moment to get my keys.'

'I'm awfully sorry about this,' Alix apologised again, aware he was looking at her nicely but closely. 'I've never lost my keys before.' Nor told so many outrageous lies.

'For safety's sake, you really ought to tape an extra set to underneath the car,' he told her.

'I'm going to,' she promised, and stepped out at the eighth floor.

The Chinese manservant opened the door, smiling benevolently.

'This young lady has lost her car keys,' Richard Kaufmann explained. 'I'm going to drive her home.'

Lee, the manservant, murmured something comforting and immediately withdrew to find the keys. He, who never went out for fear of being seen, was actually driving a young lady home. Lee realised immediately how unusual this was.

'Sit down for a moment,' Richard Kaufmann said politely. 'Maybe you would care for a drink. I know I would.'

'Just water for me,' Alix smiled, and sat down, full of a mixture of pleasant and unpleasant sensations.

The realisation that she had achieved contact didn't thrill her at all. She even had the certainty, though she didn't know why, that she could get a story out of him right now.

'I'm sure I saw you the other night, didn't I?' he asked her. 'You seem to enjoy running.'

'Oh, I do.' She accepted a glass of soda water with girlish gratitude. 'It's important to keep fit.'

He gave her another close look from under his eyelashes and splashed a dash of whisky into the soda water he had poured himself. 'I don't really care about being fit. Something else drives me.'

'Restlessness, I suppose.' She smiled at him and got up. 'After years of frantic involvement in a career, it must be difficult to just stop.'

'I haven't done anything for more than a year,' he admitted.

'But of course, you'll pick up your career again. You're a great artist. Look at all you've accomplished.'

'Still . . . still, it was not enough.' He drained his glass and set it down rather jarringly; a handsome, middle-aged man with brooding good looks.

Lee, in the doorway, seemed to have lost his animation. Probably he was used to watching his master wallow in self-pity, Alix thought. It didn't take a psychiatrist to see that Richard Kaufmann was feeling very sorry for himself, dissatisfaction twisting his fine yet slightly blurred features.

'Ah, there you are, Lee!' Kaufmann came out of his very convincing pose.

'Such a nuisance!' Alix smiled at the manservant. A lamp behind her outlined her head, the slender lightly clad body. She couldn't have looked less like the woman who had altered the whole course of his master's life.

They went down to the basement and he put her into his car. It was a silver Mercedes, but he didn't turn it very well. In fact, Alix discovered, he had no feel for fine machinery at all. Curious in a man whose whole life had been built on superb manual dexterity. There was the possibility, of course, that that hadn't been his first drink of the day.

She began to speak of his recordings she particularly liked to listen to, her comments informed and sincerely admiring. He told a wry, funny story about a concert he had once given in a bush town and they laughed together softly, achieving an easy, almost instant rapport.

When they reached Rusty's house, he briefly touched her hand. 'Please, don't let this be goodbye.' The light from the dash gave an added poignancy to his expression. He had dark eyes like Carl Danning, but oh, what a world of difference!

'It would be a pity to.' Her own expression was subtly shaded. Indeed it was difficult to tell who was suffering most.

'Shall we say dinner one evening?'

'That would be lovely.' She said it valiantly, though it was certain it would all come out about her.

'May I ring you?'

If it wasn't so sad, it would have been hilarious. She couldn't deliver a painful shock and give him *Impact*'s number, so she was forced into giving him her home number and let him wonder about the digits. 'You can reach me there over the weekend.'

'I'll call,' he said softly as she closed the door.

Briefly Alix wondered what she was going to say to the Macleans. The truth, though entertaining, was a good deal too involved. She waited in the shadows until the Mercedes turned the corner, and as it did so, another car cruised up beside her.

She got in and threw him a speaking look, surprised at her totally unexpected feeling of relief. 'It might be an idea to give Val this story. I'm feeling remorseful already.'

'Of course you are, my dear,' he laughed gently. 'I know exactly how you feel. You want to step out into the clearing, tell him you're from *Impact* and have done with it.'

'I didn't say that exactly.' It came to her forcibly that she wanted the story.

'So what are you going to do now?' He glanced at her as she pulled the rubber band from her hair.

'Gosh, that hurt!' she exclaimed.

'Are you going to tell me?'

'We're going to have dinner.'

'Tough.' He gave another laugh.

'Oh, shut up!' She shrugged miserably. 'I like him. I haven't the faintest wish to hurt him, or cause him pain.'

'So the passion was mutual?'

'No passion,' she said sharply, her grey eyes flashing. 'I must confess to a little spurt of fellow feeling and sympathy.'

'You don't think he might really want to talk?' his voice came back to her, hard and professional. 'It's my bet he can't keep it to himself any longer. I'm not so clumsy I'd send in Val. A nice, sometime sober, artistic type like that would appreciate the marked difference between you and the other members of the team. You're a young lady of distinction—not a great deal of you, but all quality. Tell the truth, if you want to, but wait until dinner is over.'

'He would never want to speak to me again.' Her hair fell forward in a silver-gilt cascade around her face.

'I've got great faith in you, Conroy,' he said. 'I'm betting he's so damned intoxicated we'll have difficulty getting his attention back to the keyboard.'

'There's no piano in the apartment,' she told him broodingly.

'I bet the neighbours are glad.'

You're a boor, Carl Danning, she thought, but wasn't game to say. 'You don't really think he *can't* play any more?'

'Who knows?' He shrugged a broad shoulder.

'Well, *I* care!'

'You're a sweet thing, though, Conroy. A sweet, sweet thing.'

'It just depresses me, that's all. I hate lies.'

'You're reacting just as I thought you would, under the circumstances. After dinner, he'll suggest you go back to the apartment. . . .'

'Did I mention that I've met the Chinese manservant?' she interrupted.

'He's promised him the day off.' He glanced at her with his black eyes. 'Don't interrupt. You'll have another coffee. Perhaps brandy, a liqueur. No piano, you say?'

'No.' She shook her head.

'Mention that you love his records.'

'I already have. Where are you taking me to, anyway?'

'Call it the long way round. There won't be any seduction scene. He's trying to impress you.'

'At any rate, you might get your story,' she said bitterly.

'Oh, for cryin' out loud!' he exclaimed brusquely. 'Why is it these poetic types tear a woman's heart?'

'I'll tell you why,' said Alix, and slammed her hand down on the console. 'They think women count too. They're sympatico.'

'Is this a personal attack?' he asked jeeringly. 'You know, I can hear what you think.'

For the first time she looked directly at him, seeing the blunt, forceful features. 'Whatever made you think I was pointing a finger at you?'

'Because you love to, Conroy. If you could make me disappear you would.'

'*Whoosh!*' She threw her hands in the air, with little or no control over herself where he was concerned.

'You little bitch!'

He said it very softly, yet it made her heart pound.

'Whatever makes you happy!' On the brink of a coup, she seemed totally unconcerned about her job, lightheaded with nerves. Vaguely she thought of Peter and what extra she could buy him with a bonus. 'Of course I didn't mean that.'

'But you definitely *did*. Of all the people who work for me, you bug me the most.'

'Well, let me say I bear you no ill will because of it.'

'Tell me that again tomorrow night.' They were approaching the park and he brought the powerful car to a halt a few feet away.

'My keys, please.' Her grey eyes seemed to glow in the dark.

'Fortunately I saw you drop them—a moment to savour.'

'I feel as though I'm in the middle of a fantasy,' she said, suddenly angry with herself.

'Enjoying it all the same!' His mouth twisted and he rid himself of her keys. 'I won't tell you I've wasted more than a couple of hours on my ghastly role.'

'I couldn't have done it single-handed,' she said briskly, and opened out the door. 'Deep down, I don't think of you too badly.'

'May I ask when you're going to do the flowers?' he demanded, his sardonic voice full of a wry humour.

'You'll see!'

'*Tell me.*' He reached out and suddenly caught her hand.

'Oh, in the morning.' There were those tremors again, rippling over her entire body.

'I'll leave the key with the caretaker.'

'You're an angel!' she responded unwisely, and shut the door.

CHAPTER FOUR

'You really are beautiful!' said Maggie, and poured herself another drink, looking around for somewhere to set it down. 'Perfect. It cuts into me to see a girl as beautiful as you.'

'Then I'd better keep carefully clear of your cooking,' returned Alix. 'It looks scrumptious!'

'How's Pete?' Maggie turned to smile at her.

'Fine. He's over at the Macleans' for the weekend.'

'A nice woman, that,' Maggie commented. 'I helped her out with her Melbourne Cup party. She mentioned you told her to call me.'

'Well, you're the best, Maggie,' Alix returned simply. 'Enough room to work in here?'

'I'll manage.' Maggie grinned impishly. Once she had been as slim as Alix, but years of sampling her own cooking, not to mention cooking for a living, had put a good deal of padding on her small frame. 'This is some apartment, isn't it? Your Mr Danning knows exactly what he wants!'

'He's not *my* Mr Danning,' Alix said seriously.

'Really?' Maggie smiled. 'I didn't think anyone could accuse *you* of being negligent.'

'He's not my kind of feller,' Alix murmured in a low tone, then she caught sight of Maggie's expression. 'Don't you believe me?'

'Of course, dear. That's why you're looking so beautiful.'

It was true. She *had* gone to a lot of trouble. In fact she had changed her dress three times before she was satisfied with her appearance. Now she wore a clinging violet silk jersey thin-strapped with diamanté and brushed her long hair out to a silken smoothness. She would be a fool if she didn't know she looked good, yet she felt edgy with nerves.

'They're going to *love* this!' said Maggie, gazing down fondly at one of her specialities, caviar aux aubergines. 'God knows I spent enough time on it, but it really is superb.'

'When are the girls coming?' Alix prepared to move off.

'In about ten minutes.' Maggie turned to check the oven temperature. 'You go off and enjoy yourself. And by the way, kid, thanks for getting me the job.'

By seven-thirty, everyone had arrived, and after a couple of pre-dinner drinks they all took their places at the table.

'What a perfect spot!' the Senator said graciously, his eyes not on the dazzling night-time view, but Alix's face.

'Great! I wish I could pack it up and take it home.' Danny Kirby, the pop singer, seconded with marked vivacity. 'The only trouble is I'd never be there to enjoy it.'

'No performing artist is a free soul,' Carl Danning pointed out. 'Constant travel is just part of the job.'

'A case of either do it or quit,' Danny said laconically. 'I've worked too hard to quit now.'

'I hope later you're going to give us a song,' Alix said kindly. She had seen him arrive with his guitar.

'I'd be delighted!' He smiled at her so nicely, Alix

began to like him. It was true she had written him off as inconsequential even before they had met, but it wasn't fair to judge him as a person who simply didn't please her as an entertainer.

Maggie's staff came in to serve the first course and the conversation became general. The rather too voluptuous redhead on Danning's left extended her hand to stroke his sleeve lightly and said something that made him laugh.

Her husband would never be through keeping tabs on her, Alix thought waspishly. At least he knew where she was tonight, from her vantage point across the table. She had to be somewhere in her late thirties and the form-fitting turquoise blue gown was too tight, but she was a very attractive woman with a decided look of sexuality. An odd choice, perhaps, for her serious, thoughtful, bespectacled husband, Max Schofield, the top columnist.

By the time they were through a superb beef dish served with various accompaniments, it dawned on Alix that the Senator was trying to charm her. She had been far too busy watching Danning and Roberta Schofield out of the corner of her eye. Flirting, quite openly.

'I've never been interviewed by a woman,' he said. 'How would you like the job?'

'I'm sure it would improve our circulation,' she smiled at him, more alluringly than she ever intended—a side effect of watching Roberta.

'I'll speak to Carl about it,' the Senator promised, and fingered his wine glass. 'Carl was telling me you're John Conroy's daughter. I greatly admired your father's work.'

'He was the best!' Alix said simply, not wishing to talk freely of her father. It hurt too much.

'Of course I've dined at the Wainwright place,' the Senator told her, apparently insensitive to atmosphere. 'A remarkable house, like a modern castle. It was just made for its site.'

'Yes, they all were.' Alix glanced down the table, across the beautiful centrepiece of white roses and the Georgian candlesticks, to find Carl Danning's black, brilliant eyes unexpectedly on her.

'They tell me your old home is on the market—or it very soon will be,' the Senator continued, jarring her back to attention.

'So I've heard.' She made a rather pathetic little gesture with her hand, a kind of warding off, but it was a sheer waste of time.

'I believe Carl's got a few plans there!' the Senator leaned towards her confidentially, nodding his silver-winged dark head. 'He wants a *real* place, somewhere he can spread out and have an out-of-doors. His own private world.'

'Then he's kept it pretty quiet,' she said almost curtly, but the Senator scarcely even heard.

'Brilliant chap, Danning. The kind of man you want on your team.' He took a quick look down the table. 'First thing I want to do is get him off your magazine. A man like that has got too much to offer. I'm concerned that we're not getting the benefit of his brain and dedication. The P.M. agrees. He was a Rhodes scholar—did you know that?'

'No, I didn't,' Alix said, and let it go at that.

'Brilliant! Started life in an orphanage, adopted, parents killed, back to the orphanage. Carl's is a real success story, and I like to think I discovered him. We've been friends for years now.'

By the end of dinner, Alix thought tersely, all Carl Danning's secrets would be laid bare. She was struggling to take in what the Senator had told her. He couldn't possibly be thinking of buying her old home; it would be too terrible. She couldn't bear to think of him there. The sound of the Senator's voice started to blur. Talking, it seemed, came too easily to him.

For the dessert, Maggie had concocted a towering pyramid of tiny choux puffs, filled with cream and dipped in toffee, the top crowned with a web of finely spun sugar.

'I *shouldn't*!' Roberta protested, and allowed herself to be served.

Alix caught the eye of one of the other women guests and was amused to see that she allowed her eyes to roll very slightly.

'I'm always telling myself I'll go on a diet,' Roberta said, 'but I never do.'

'I can promise you you don't need to,' Carl Danning said gallantly, and gave her a brief, sidelong smile.

'You're making my job difficult, Carl,' Max complained. 'I'll never get her to stick to a diet now.'

'My mum used to make something like this,' Danny told them. 'Not done up all fancy but something like it. We always had a treat once a week.'

'You sound as if you were a very happy family,' Alix smiled at him.

'Oh, we were!' Danny decided to be honest. '*After* Mum and Dad got their divorce. Me and me brothers used to sing to drown out their fights. It was easier when Mum bought me a guitar. Now I'm able to do something for her. I bought her a very swanky home unit the other day. She didn't want a house—told me she'd feel nervous.'

'What car are you driving now?' Max Schofield asked him cheerfully.

'A Rolls like everybody else,' Danny grinned. 'I always feel I'd better enjoy myself now before I'm poor again.'

'If you take my advice,' Carl said to him, 'you won't *have* to be.'

'Ah, Mr Danning. . . .' Danny shrugged his narrow shoulders.

'Let us in on it,' Dave Jackson, from one of the television stations, looked interested.

'I understand Mr Danning is going to make me sing for my supper.' Danny stared down into his wine glass for a few seconds, then finished the contents off.

'Oh, splendid!' Roberta cried, and very nearly snorted.

It was deliberately unkind and no one appeared to appreciate it, including Danning. Alix saw him look at Roberta for a few seconds, then away again. He could crush anyone with a glance.

They moved away from the dining table to have coffee and liqueurs while Maggie and her girls very deftly tidied up the disarray. It had been an excellent meal and everyone looked very mellow and at ease.

Roberta wanted to gossip and she did, in fact, drop two startling news items, despite her husband's attempts to stop her, before Carl Danning, playing a very charming and urbane host, led the conversation to better things.

No one seemed to want to go home, and Alix swallowed a Scotch down without thinking. The Senator's news had just appalled her, and though she appeared to be enjoying herself as much as anyone else. She was frightened of what she might say to him afterwards.

When Carl asked Danny to sing, he did so without hesitation; only it wasn't the Danny Kirby any of them knew at all. He sang a slow, sad ballad he had written himself, all about lost love, but he sang it as though no one had ever said it all before ... his bleached fair head hung over his guitar, his long, thin fingers picking out beautiful chords. Even his voice was different, a true voice, not big in tone, but round and resonant.

When he finished there was a moment of complete silence as though they were all wrapped in a spell. Then Carl put his hands together.

'I give you the *real* Danny Kirby!'

Immediately everyone seemed released. 'That was beautiful!' Alix complimented him warmly.

'You really liked it?'

'I'd like you to sing again,' she said quietly.

Carl nodded and Danny launched into another one of his own songs, displaying a talent that none of his fans had ever seen. As the up-and-coming king of pop he had developed, with the aid of boom microphones, an ear-splitting style, so his performance now seemed all that much more incredible.

He finished off unselfconsciously and smiled at them, and Max Schofield spoke up for them all: 'If I were you, son, I'd listen to Carl's advice. You'll find a wide audience with songs like that. What's more, you won't ruin your vocal chords.'

Danny's surprise performance, obviously planned by their host, topped off a very enjoyable evening. By one o'clock they had all gone home, Roberta snuggling up to her husband, after she had just kissed Carl long and lingeringly on the mouth.

Careful, Alix warned herself. Stay cool. She didn't even want to think about what she had learned tonight. Maggie had gone off richly rewarded and it was time now to take herself off. She had done her duty and that was that.

'Is this what you're looking for?' Danning asked, and held up her glittering little evening purse.

'Yes, thank you,' she said sternly.

'One gets the feeling you've got something on your mind.' Instead of handing her the purse, he put it down again.

'No, nothing!' She shook her gleaming head.

'Do you mean you're going to wait to tell me about it?' He loosened the collar of his beautiful shirt and pulled down the tie.

'The time has come to go home,' she said firmly. 'You've seen off your friends. Now you can walk me to my car.'

'Oh, how you hurt me!' he hit his heart. 'A girl like you is death to my ego!'

'Surely not, after Roberta's goodbye.' Her grey eyes had picked up some of the colour from her dress and they looked lilac.

'Roberta needs constant proof that she's still a highly desirable woman.'

'Then you know well how to keep her happy.'

'Quiet, Conroy. Don't be bitchy. Sit down again and be still.'

'I want to go home,' she said. 'Peter looks out for me.'

'No doubt he does when he's home,' he said pointedly. 'Don't look so surprised,' he added, watching her, 'Maggie told me he was spending the weekend with friends. The same friends so conveniently to hand last night.'

'So I still want to go,' she said, more like an angry child than the lovely, poised young woman she had appeared all night.

'You look very nice,' he said blandly, and lowered himself into an armchair. 'I always thought grey eyes were ordinary, but yours seem to pick up colour from everything you wear. I've seen them blue and green and silver, now they're hyacinth.'

She didn't answer but picked up her purse.

'I hate to see you go,' he said in that mocking, dark tone.

'If you want to walk to the car with me,' she said a little grandly, 'you can.'

'Aren't you going to stay and clean up?'

'Maggie has done it all.' She seemed to be shaking inside, her nerves fluttering. 'Please let's go!'

'Of course.' He stood up, a big man, hard and tough. Some might call him dynamic; Alix preferred to call him tough, as all his concentration was first on survival, then afterwards, success. His childhood must have been extremely difficult. An uprooted orphan. Blame it all on his childhood.

He walked towards her, looking as though she was speaking all her thoughts into a tape recorder, and all of a sudden she began to tremble. The tremors on the outside, not locked up at all. His eyes were fixed on her, black as hell, and she backed right up against the door.

'You goddamn little fool!'

The way he said it left her in no doubt he was angry.

She moved her lips to speak, but somehow she couldn't. I've got you where I want you. Now see how good you are, Conroy. He was all around her, the raw power and the maleness, so magnetic, she had to admit to her own helplessness.

'I've been waiting to kiss you for too long,' he challenged her openly with more hostility than ardour.

'You might consider I don't want you to.'

'Liar.' His hands reached for her, spanned her waist, then fell to grasp her by her narrow hips. 'It's the same for you. The thing you've always evaded.'

She wasn't ready yet to make any concession towards honesty. 'You've got it all wrong,' she said sarcastically, bouncing back fast.

'How much did Lew tell you?' The black eyes probed her face.

'Among other things, that you were planning to buy our old home.'

'And you can't stand it, can you?'

'So why talk about it?'

She was seething with a wild impatience, the colour lighting up her skin.

'Because we've got to. Don't you see that?'

Alix was genuinely taken aback and it made her all that more furiously impatient. She had always feared him, feared he would disturb her life—worse, ruin it. She had been fighting him really from the very first day. The thought made her try to recoil, but he drew her even closer, with overwhelming strength.

'Well, Alix,' he said deliberately, 'let's try and clear up the first mystery.'

Every nerve in her body clamoured outrage, but for an instant she was without will. When she should have been screaming she turned up her mouth to a man she detested, and he caught her almost savagely into his arms, covering her sweet, fragrant mouth with his own.

The shock was chaotic, literally robbing her of breath. He was so much stronger, so much more positive, demanding, that she felt her knees buckle under her.

'*Alix!*' he muttered, and desire was deep in his eyes.

She couldn't cry out or even speak, and he lifted her in his arms with great ease and walked back with her to the sofa. She simply didn't know what to do to stop him and his hand came under her chin, holding her mouth to him.

It was a curse; it had to be—this fire in the blood. In the shock and excitement her face had lost all colour, and Carl twined his hand through her long hair so she couldn't turn her head away.

Eventually the kissing, voluptuous though it was, didn't seem enough, and he groaned softly, almost in anguish, and lowered his hand to her breast, seeking the warm, satin flesh.

Where am I? she thought. Where *am* I? It was frightening how easily he had invaded her inviolate self. She wanted to pull his hand fiercely away from her, but her whole body was quickening, quivering, sighing, yielding. . . .

Nothing in her experience had prepared her for passion; the thunderous, wicked longing. She wanted him to touch her, not just her breasts, but all over. She *wanted* to feel this terrible, exquisite stirring. What a tragedy!

The subdued golden glow of the lighting fell on her violet dress, white velvety skin, young breasts rising purely like sculptured alabaster. Nothing in the world so beautiful as a woman's body. She didn't want to see his face, this ravisher, but she knew now she craved him.

'Don't cry!' she heard him say.

Was she crying? She should be. There was a limit to what she should be expected to take. What was the good of disciplining her mind when she went to pieces when he touched her?

Fleetingly the starch was back in her and she tried to close her mouth to the perfect, cruel exploration. She couldn't bear it any longer, this loss of her self.

'Kiss me,' he said almost violently. 'Kiss me.'

Her closed eyes flew open and she stared into the taut, dark face looming over her. 'Not now. Not *ever*. Not of my own free will!'

It was bravado at its most blatant, but incredibly Carl didn't seem to know.

His mouth moved soundlessly in an angry laugh and he lowered his head again, a masterly revenge, thinking perhaps that possession was better than nothing. She could be broken; he would know that from her deep trembling.

So often in her mad fantasies about him, she had imagined him kissing her, but she had never thought to feel the terrible agony inside, the unsatiated, raging craving. The hell of being a woman, wanting to be loved, to be made love to, every shred of camouflage stripped away from her.

She didn't know she was making sounds like a whimpering kitten, sounds that were driving him crazy, until with a great surge of frustrated passion he put her violently away from him.

'If I don't get you home now,' he said tightly, 'I'm taking you to bed.'

Robbed of his support, Alix fell back completely against his sofa. 'Then it's definitely home!' she cried out intensely. There was no other answer. He didn't love her. She didn't love him, and now that he had released her she could at least reason again. Sex without love really shocked her to the very core.

'I must go,' she said, but still she couldn't stand up. Her young girl's body had a spontaneous, abandoned look, strangely innocent yet extremely seductive. She simply couldn't come to terms with the crazy ambivalence of her feelings—feelings she knew would plague her from now on. This was a tremendous thing for her; after all, God help her, she was a virgin with a natural fear of her own emotions, when Carl Danning probably had had multitudes of women.

'*God!*' she said aloud, and in the profound silence it sounded like a plea for forgiveness.

'So now you're hating yourself,' he said, understanding at once.

'I really would have fought you with my last breath.'

'Oh, I believe you, darling. I *do*.'

He leant over her and one hand brushed her cheek as he smoothed the long golden strands of hair away from her flushed face. 'I have to take you home, Conroy.' His voice was husky, even tender. He looked as if she was really important to him.

Desire came back like the deluge, wave after wave of it, rolling over her. She had only to lift a hand for him to carry her into his bedroom, lay her down on that black quilted satin, pull off her dress. She could see them both clearly. Carl had a magnificent body, curly dark hair on his chest. They seemed to fit beautifully together—but then he would be devastating with any woman.

Resolutely she adjusted the diamanté straps of her dress and sat up. How could she ever keep up the cool don't-touch-me again? Momentarily she had the dark, morbid desire to jump off the nearest bridge. She knew his methods as well as anybody. All his dinner parties ended in a flood of passion; it was just so humiliating it had to be her.

'Little fool,' he said gently, and took hold of her two hands, 'stop giving yourself hell.'

'It won't change anything, will it?' her eyes defied him to disagree.

'Little worry on that score,' he said dryly.

His words seemed to comfort her. At least he had had the decency to let her up. In fact, all things considered, he had acted with more restraint than she had. The very thought was sobering.

'You don't look happy,' he said.

'I was engaged once,' she told him in a wondering voice.

'Hard as it is to believe now.' He took her face in his two hands and brushed another kiss across her mouth.

'Strange,' she said, her grey eyes lost in thought.

'I take it he wasn't a terribly ardent fellow?'

'I don't really know.' She continued to stare up at him. 'He kissed me, of course.'

'And?'

'I haven't even got a picture of him in my mind.'

'Don't worry about it,' he said lightly, and dropped his hands to her shoulders.

'But I could have *married* him.'

'I don't think so,' he said comfortably, 'you're a very intelligent girl.'

'That doesn't seem very important at the moment.' She looked away from his brilliant, searching eyes. 'Have you *really* wanted to kiss me?'

'That's right, Conroy.' He turned her very gently to the door. 'I'm a savage.'

'You're not like anyone else I know.'

He smiled without offence and switched off all but one light.

'What are you doing that for?' She looked up at him curiously.

'I'm taking you home. Isn't that nice of me?'

'I'll go the same way I got here,' she said valiantly, 'in my car.'

'I don't think so,' he said. 'I'll drop it over to you tomorrow.'

'You mean you think I'm not in a fit state to drive?'

'I don't want to worry about it.' He ran his eyes over her lovely, dazed face. 'Besides, just occasionally I like to see you a little lost. Cool, alert Conroy, helpless like a little girl.'

In the car, she nearly fell asleep, and when she

came back to the present, his lips were at her throat.

'Wake up, Sleeping Princess!'

She had the insane longing to ask him to stay the night, give in to her terrible temptations. At least she would know what it was like to be made love to by a past master of the art. And *art* it was, plus a powerful chemistry. Unlike charges attract—she went back to her schoolgirl science.

'That was very kind of you,' she said. 'Perhaps you've some other scheme afoot?'

'I was under the impression we'd done very well for one night,' he answered, his voice rife with mockery. 'Stay there. I'll come round for you.'

'Lovely!' She was almost back to her cool, flippant self.

He helped her out of the car and put an arm around her. 'Am I to understand your fiancé never lost his head?'

'No.' She looked up at him. 'You're to understand I never lost my mine.'

They went into the block of units and Carl not only put her in the lift but delivered her to her door.

'Good night, Conroy,' he looked down at her with his heavily fringed black eyes. 'I'm going home to write in my diary.'

'You'll probably finish up selling the screen rights.' They were back to shadow dancing around one another, only this time with a grain of affection.

'I'd like to meet your brother,' he said.

'Well, that can be arranged.' Alix slumped and he leaned forward to kiss her forehead lightly.

'Go to bed. I'll bring your car over tomorrow.'

'Carl?' For the first time ever she said his christian name and saw his face change; muscles tightening under the skin, brilliant eyes narrowing, tension in the powerfully built body.

'You've taken a hell of a long time to say that.'

'I only want to thank you for a really nice evening.' Her silvery grey eyes were still sheened with lilac. 'If you want to meet Peter why don't you share a meal with us tomorrow evening? I have to pick him up at Rusty's late afternoon. We could have something here.'

'In that case I'll accept before you change your mind. Better, I'll pick him up and bring him and the car home for you. Unless you want it?'

'No.' She had done all the shopping. She shook her golden head, her fingers clinging to her temple. 'I swear I don't know what's wrong with me!'

'Perhaps you're facing a few things you've always denied.' It wasn't clear whether he was being mocking, sarcastic, or what. He saluted her briefly putting his right hand to his head, looking big and rugged and extraordinarily aggressive. 'If everything's in order, then, I'll go.'

'Aye, aye, sir!' She looked up at him and blinked. Now that she thought about it, he did have a swashbuckling look about him, the terrible pirate naturally adept at ravishing women. 'I'll ring Peter and tell him.'

'Good.' He gave her another brief nod, then he was gone.

Alix closed the door, walked through the empty apartment and looked through the window. In her humble opinion, nothing was in order at all.

In the morning light, she went over the evening again. It was incredible, the whole thing. She vacuumed and polished and dusted, made a creamy chicken casserole and Peter's favourite chocolate cake, all the while muttering and murmuring and sighing aloud. It was clear she was under some kind of a spell, but a further dose of Danning would cure her.

Damn! she couldn't even think of him as Danning any more. How curious the change in him when she had said his name. He was an interesting man really, very complex. She worked so hard, bent over squeeze mop and vacuum cleaner, she decided to wash her hair again.

Oh, wake up to yourself, Conroy! she said to her reflection in the bathroom mirror. There wasn't the slightest doubt she was physically in his power, but as he had remarked himself, she was very intelligent. Well . . . fairly intelligent. She pinned her long hair on top of her head and stepped under the strong jet of water. If it wasn't coming out like Niagara, it gave a ghastly trickle.

Towards mid-afternoon, when she was sunning herself out on the balcony, still obsessively mooning over the night before, the phone rang.

'Hello,' she said, frightened it might be something wrong with Peter. She didn't need to have a reason. She always worried and would continue to worry for a long time.

'Alix?' a voice asked, vaguely familiar.

'Yes.' Come along, then, she thought, say what you want.

'Richard Kaufmann.'

'Of course.' She injected a good deal more friendliness into her voice. Strictly speaking she had forgotten he even existed. 'How are you?'

'Fine, and you?'

'Very well.' She drooped down on a chair. 'I'm glad you rang. I was melting out on the balcony.'

'Such a lovely day.'

'Yes.' She glanced down at her watch. They could quite easily arrive early; she had told Peter any time after four.

'Why I've rung,' Richard explained in his gentle, cultured tone, 'is to ask you if we can meet some time. I go out so rarely these days, but I thought we might have dinner.'

So his attitude of non-participation was getting to him! 'I'd like that,' she heard herself saying. 'In fact, Mr Kaufmann, I'm honoured.'

'Oh, *Richard*, please!'

'Richard.' She imagined him pouring himself a drink, watching the bubbles.

'Any place particular you would like?' He underlined the words very gently so she knew perfectly well he wanted it to be very private.

'What about the Ambassador?' Nothing more exclusive or discreet than that.

They arranged a date for mid-week and Alix told him she would meet him there, citing a function she had to pop in on round about six o'clock. In actual fact, she did have to go, so it lessened her guilt feelings.

He didn't linger chatting after that and Alix put the receiver down like a girl in a trance. She was in a position to win an interview with the great Richard Kaufmann, yet she couldn't seem to savour it at all.

Let all the other journalists eat their hearts out, she felt in her bones she could get him to talk to her; not only as a woman to whom he might be attracted, but as a reporter. Indeed, once started, he might be difficult to stop.

It was approaching four-thirty before Carl and Peter arrived. Alix's elbows were already sore from leaning over the balcony, and as she peered down at them, she could see they were laughing. Which was all right except that she didn't really want Peter to like Carl. What she was doing was setting up various emotional mechanisms to prevent her from going any further. She knew now, given half a chance, Carl Danning would push her to the limit, and her susceptibility was real enough to make strong defensive plans.

As it turned out, their little dinner party was quite an occasion. Alix couldn't remember when she had seen Peter more animated and happy than when he had been with their dear father. Of course Danning (she was back to calling him Danning) was putting himself out to be charming and Peter, in turn, was making a big fuss of their guest.

It nearly broke her heart.

Peter talked and he talked and he talked, insisting on making the coffee for them himself, and far from looking bored, Carl Danning encouraged the boy to tell him all about his school and his friends, his plans and ambitions. Peter even made him sit down and go through picture albums, able it seemed to allow this stranger to intrude on their most private life.

Alix didn't look. She couldn't bear to look at pictures of her father and mother, but in some peculiar way Carl appeared to be helping Peter; saying all the right things, supportive, she supposed, and *real*, and it obviously pleased and relieved Peter to be able to speak so calmly and lovingly of his parents at last.

Alix had nothing to say. She crossed the room to get herself another cup of coffee. If Carl had deliberately set out to impress and befriend Peter he couldn't have acted more suitably. Peter, in turn, was highly intelligent and by no means easy to fool. He really liked and respected their guest, and Alix had to remember that Carl Danning was pretty damned clever himself. Rhodes scholar, granted. But surely Peter didn't have to make that much of a fuss of him?

'I'm showing Carl some pictures of you,' Peter called out to her. 'The whole album to yourself.'

'Oh, for heaven's sake!'

Peter chortled. 'Would you mind terribly if I told Carl that funny story about how you got bitten by a snake?'

'Don't you dare!'

'She went mad, quite mad,' Peter broke the story down almost reluctantly. 'Of course it wasn't a snake at all. Alix had always been one for a bit of drama.'

She made a little face and Danning smiled at her suddenly. 'Isn't that the way it is?' he said dryly.

If he expected her to smile back, she didn't, but her heart gave an odd little flutter. He had a very good mouth and teeth, and she had rarely seen him smile.

Down in the street a dog barked and Peter suddenly said, 'We had to give away our beautiful labrador, did you know? He was that rare chocolate colour.'

'The Allens gave him a good home,' Alix answered,

rather emotionally. To this day she missed Rolly.

'I wish we could have a dog.' Peter dug a hand into his soft fair hair. 'If you have a close relationship with a family pet, you always want one.'

The moment threatened to become emotional, so Carl produced a very funny story about the tough old bull terrier who had been a guard dog at the orphanage. Peter wasn't at all surprised at the mention of an orphanage, so Alix concluded, quite correctly, that Carl had told her young brother something of his early days on their way home.

Later on, after their guest had gone home, Peter confirmed it.

'He's a pretty remarkable man, isn't he?' he said admiringly. 'It must have been terribly tough on him as a kid. He must have had to really fight for survival. His adopted parents were killed, did you know that?'

'I have been told,' said Alix. She started to wash up and Peter picked up a towel.

'I can't understand why you don't like him,' Peter frowned down at their best plates. 'Maybe you don't know him very well.'

'Perhaps I don't.' Alix was forced to concede the truth. 'I used to think he was terribly tough and aggressive.'

'Well, I suppose he *is*,' said Peter, almost defensively. 'Wouldn't *you* be? We had such a good life. He must have had nothing, except for a little while, then it was all taken from him again. He told me that, even as a kid, he was very ambitious.'

'I'll bet!' said Alix.

'I found him terribly interesting.' Peter yanked out a chair and sat down to wipe up.

'Then I'm glad!' Because she loved her brother so much, Alix turned her head to smile at him. 'Further, I'm quite sure he liked you.'

'I didn't talk too much, did I?' Peter asked a little anxiously.

'Yes, indeed you did, but it was all very enjoyable.'

'I'm sorry.'

Alix leant over and kissed him on the forehead. 'Nothing to be sorry about. I thought you behaved beautifully. I'm very proud of you.

'I think he likes you,' Peter pointed out with a boyish lack of subtlety.

'That's nice.' Alix took off her rubber gloves with a gesture of unconcern. 'Please remember, dear, the only thing he's ever likely to be, is my boss.'

'Anyway, he's a real *man*!' Peter declared, and hung up the tea towel neatly. 'They're not too easy to come by these days.'

Curiously enough, Alix was thinking the same thing. Half her chaste resistance was to Carl's blatant masculinity. She had had enough of Carl Danning for one night. 'You haven't said anything about what you did over at Rusty's?' She looked at her young brother enquiringly, noting that already his wrists were sticking out of an almost new shirt.

'Let me think.' Started on talking, Peter slipped sideways over the arm of the sofa and launched into a full account.

CHAPTER FIVE

First thing Monday morning, Carl sent for Alix.

'I'm taking you off the Kaufmann assignment,' he said, flipping through a rival magazine.

'You're what?'

He frowned and looked quickly over at her. 'Your hearing okay?'

'Damn it, you *can't*!' She was taken utterly by surprise.

'Could you repeat that, Conroy?' His squarish dark face was expressionless.

'What's going on here?' she demanded. 'Has Val been speaking to you?'

'If she did, I didn't take any notice of it.'

'Then why the change of plan? Are you going to drop it altogether?'

'No, I'm not.' He gazed at her a while with his black eyes. 'I've decided to be honest with you, Conroy. I realise now I made a mistake giving you the Kaufmann assignment. I fear it might be too much for you to handle.'

Alix drew in her breath sharply, trying to relax. There would be no point at all in losing her temper. 'I don't think I told you I'm having dinner with him this coming Wednesday.'

'No, you didn't tell me,' he said curtly. 'When did this happen?'

'He rang yesterday.'

'Which makes it even plainer, it's my duty to protect you.'

'You're joking!' She looked at him incredulously, brought up short by his tone. 'I'm on the verge of a coup and you want me to just melt away. I won't do it!'

'Everyone else around here does what they're told.'

'Oh, *please*, Carl,' her grey eyes shone with endeavour, 'Let me prove I can get an interview out of him.'

'Why him in particular?' he asked shortly.

'I just don't understand!' her young face looked bewildered. 'You were the one who set it all up. We're looking for a big story for Christmas. Maybe you remember yourself talking pictures?'

'I never expected it to go beyond the bounds of duty.' He got up and walked to the plate glass window. 'I don't think I need point out that this man had a reputation—and I don't mean as a pianist.'

'God,' she said heatedly, 'I'm not thinking of being his mistress.'

'Could be I never realised how innocent and vulnerable you really are.'

'What rubbish!' She felt frustrated. 'I tell you, he's a gentleman.'

'Which means you found him attractive?' He turned around and looked at her.

'I guess I did. He's the kind of man women would always find attractive.'

'Oh, I appreciate that,' he answered dryly. 'When are you going to explain the situation to him?'

'That depends,' she said vaguely, worried by the grimness of his expression.

'I think I'd like to know now.'

'I'm just going to feel my way.' She kept her voice low when it felt like rising out of control. 'I appreciate your concern, but I just don't understand it. I know perfectly well how to behave in any given situation.'

'It's not *your* behaviour that's troubling my sleep,' he said sharply. 'You go out to dinner if you like, but don't you dare step into his apartment.'

'Whatever you say.' She sat back and stared up at him a little helplessly. 'Are you on to some kind of privileged information? He's not Jack the Ripper or anything like that?'

'Up until the time he married Crespi, he was rarely without some woman or other. She pulled him into line until it all began to go flat. My educated guess is, he's ready for comfort.'

'I thought you didn't care how you got your story,' Alix challenged him.

As soon as she said it she knew she had made a terrible mistake. Carl started to move towards her and she shut her eyes and held her breath. This must be how the French aristocrats felt before they got the chop.

'I just hope you realise,' he said softly, 'that another crack like that will find you out of a job.'

'I want to apologise!' She'd be a damned fool if she didn't.

He was facing her, leaning against the desk. 'Was it worth it, Conroy?'

'Joe used to call you a tiger,' she said. 'I guess a lot of things he said about you weren't true, but he was angry and frightened and jealous.'

'Hey, hold it,' he said mockingly. 'I thought you worshipped poor old Joe. Father figure and all that!'

'Not me,' she said. 'I just liked him, that's all. We all did.'

'You want my hanky?'

Alix swung up in disgust and he reached out and held her wrist. '*I* decide when the meetings are over.'

'You're hurting me!' She put her hand over his and tried to loosen his grip.

'Do you want to tell me what restaurant you're going to?' His grasp slackened, but he didn't let her go.

'The Ambassador.' She tilted her chin and looked him full in the eye. 'You're not thinking of sending the F.B.I.?'

'That little bit of sarcasm isn't needed,' he said shortly. 'Tell him halfway through dinner. Tell him it's okay if you don't finish. You're the sort of girl who could melt a heart of stone.'

'Thank you.' She accepted it laconically. 'What happens if he shows signs of forgiveness? He could decide to give me a story there and then.'

'Tell him one has to put it all on a tape-recorder. If he shows any sign of wavering, tell him he owes it to his public. Even the most trivial details would be great copy. Suggest to him that he can't bottle it up any longer. Let him see himself pictured on the front cover. Lennie could take some terrific shots, something grandiose, something our women readers will love!'

'I'll do my best,' she sighed.

'Just don't try taking any short cuts. As I told you he's the classic little-boy-lost.'

When Alix got back to her desk, she told Gary at once.

'Maybe he's looking for another Crespi, or a reasonable facsimile.'

'Well, he'd better not look at me!' Alix answered directly. 'Anyway, I know exactly how old he is. He's forty-eight.'

'A mere child!' Gary laughted. 'I know dozens of men with young wives.'

'He's not interested in me, Gary.' Alix looked at him pensively.

'*Aha!*' said Gary. 'So what's his motive? I mean, why does a man ask a woman out to dinner?'

'Maybe he doesn't eat regular meals. Or he's getting sick of his own company.'

'Have a care, dearie,' Gary cautioned.

'Danning doesn't want me to go.'

Gary opened his eyes wide and swung around in his chair. 'Would you mind repeating that?'

'Once is enough.'

'Well, think of that!' Gary wheeled around to the typewriter again. 'How did it go the other night?'

'Very well.'

'Look out,' said Gary suddenly, interrupting, 'here comes your most bitter rival.'

It was Val.

'Good morning.'

'Exactly.' Gary looked up at her and smiled. 'Come to play some more childish tricks?'

'You know damn well it was an accident,' Val said coldly.

'You old liar!'

'Can't deliver on the Kaufmann story?' Val turned to stare at Alix.

'Can't get past his guard dog.'

'Where does he live?' Val asked quickly.

'Oh, it's a wonderful place. You can only get there by plane.'

For an instant Val stared into the younger girl's face, tawny eyes wide, then she snarled: '*Funny!*'

'Now, now, Val,' Gary spoke up soothingly, 'you can't blame Alix for wanting to keep it to herself. A great story is involved.'

'She'll never get it! I'm absolutely sure about that. He sent Judy Garrett away, and she's the top woman journalist in the country.'

'Come on now,' Gary challenged her. 'Why, I read your fabulous thing. What was it? I know it had a lot of local colour.'

'Was it the piece I did on Fiji?' Val asked, completely taken in.

'Fabulous!' Gary told her.

'If anyone wants me,' said Alix, 'I'm going to see Len.' Len was their best photographer and he liked to plan things in advance.

'I think I might be able to bring off an interview with Richard Kaufmann,' Alix told him when she was admitted to his office.

'Good for you!' Len stopped riffling through a batch of glossies. 'We could make him personality of the year.'

'Danning wants a shot of him on our Christmas cover.'

'For that matter so does the *Women's Weekly*!' Len seemed amused. 'I take it you've achieved contact?'

'He doesn't know who I am yet.'

'You awful girl!'

'You know how it is,' Alix shrugged. 'Anyway, I'm having dinner with him Wednesday night.'

'Alone?' Len turned to stare at her.

'Of course alone,' said Alix.

'Incredible!' Len seemed amazed. 'He's had the media dogging his heels since he arrived back in the country, and it's taken our own little Alix!'

'Actually I'm sort of nervous about it,' she confessed, then broke off as she caught sight of someone standing just outside the door. 'Just a minute,' she said to Len, and sprang to her feet. 'All right, Val,' she called, 'were you spying?'

'You stupid creature!' Val looked disdainful.

'Take it calmly, girls,' Len moved into the passageway to advise. 'Can I help you, Val?' He too was annoyed, but he wasn't going to show it.

'I just wanted to compliment you on this month's selection of photographs.'

'You did that a couple of days ago.'

'You'd need an I.Q. below zero not to be awake to you,' Alix said squarely. 'This is *my* assignment, Val!'

'Who said anything about your assignment?' Val opened her eyes wide.

'I'll come back later,' Alix nodded to Len. 'When the coast is clear.' Val was capable of turning every little shred of information to her advantage, even of stealing the interview.

On the Wednesday she wore one of those little dresses that went everywhere and after work added the long, superb string of her mother's pearls. They swung almost to her waist, a lustrous reminder of the great love that had existed between her mother and father. These had been her father's wedding present to her mother and she would never part with them ever. The gold and pearl earrings she had bought herself, and as she screwed them on she debated whether to leave her hair in the smooth upturned roll she had worn all day, or let it out. Men seemed to like flowing hair and she supposed it would give her that much more of an evening look. Her hair was one of her greatest assets, and when she was ready she thought she looked pretty glamorous.

She was just tiptoeing through the office when Carl Danning swung through the glass doors.

'Well,' he said to her like a strict, because he had to be, parent, 'Let's have a look at you.'

'Does it ease your mind in some way?' She turned around and struck a model's pose.

He looked the full length of her from her head to her toes, as a general might at a soldier on an inspection line, then he said snappily: 'It's too obvious.'

'I beg your pardon!' She felt an astonishing wave of disappointment and injustice.

'It might have been an idea to leave your hair up.'

'I shall wear my hair precisely how it pleases me.'

'Then don't be surprised if you have to call for help.'

Resentments die hard. Alix was still fuming over his incredible cheek when she arrived at the gallery, but this didn't prevent her from having a thoroughly enjoyable time. One of the talented young artists whose work was on display, Susan Heathwood, had been a good friend since kindergarten days and now she was just starting to be recognised. Alix was writing a little piece on her, not as an art critic but as a contemporary delving into personality and talent.

Fifteen minutes before she was due to leave, a little conniving on somebody's part delivered a surprise. As she turned away from a little group of Susan's friends, still laughing, a personable young man with a thin, intelligent face put out his hand to her.

'*Alix!*'

For an instant she felt very much like walking past him, but there was a diffidence in his expression that made her pause. 'Hello, Guy.'

'How wonderful to run into you!'

'Is it?' she asked dryly.

'Of course it is.' He took her arm and moved her to one side. 'Well, actually, Sue happened to mention to Rosemary that you were going to do a piece on her.'

'So our little meeting was planned.'

'Why so bitter?' He stared intensely into her eyes.

'Bitter?' She lifted her eyebrows and laughed. 'Actually, Guy, I've quite forgiven you.'

'If I could only believe that!'

'You always were a conceited ass.' She began to move away from him, but he followed her.

'Please allow me to speak to you, Alix. You can't know how I've missed you.'

'Don't want to know.' She didn't even glance at his dispirited face. Once she had thought herself in love with this rather handsome young man, and though he still presented an attractive picture she was stuck with the feeling he looked rather like a tailor's dummy. He had no aura, charisma, pulsating vitality. Camilla Armstrong had actually done her a big favour.

Guy drew in his breath beside her with a little gasp. 'You used never to be cruel.'

'And I don't want to be now.' She stopped and looked full at him. 'What is it you want of me, Guy? A blessing? Are you and dear Camilla to be married?'

'Camilla isn't, never was and never will be a patch on you,' he said vehemently.

'But oh, she's got money!'

'She never looks a million like you!' Guy's eyes fell to her mother's pearls with a martyred look.

'What are we talking about anyway?' she asked kindly.

'I want to see you again.'

'Just like that?'

'Yes.' His pale blue eyes burned. 'Oh, for God's sake, Alix, yesterday was bad, but we've got tomorrow to think about.'

'Surely I haven't got a rich aunty that's died?' She held a hand to her head, trying to think of one.

'I suppose I deserve that!'

Alix shook her golden head slowly, but not in denial. 'Just lately I've been wondering how I ever got engaged to you. Mummy and Daddy weren't happy about it, I knew that in my bones.'

'They thought I wasn't good enough for you.'

'The more I think about it, the more I think they were right!'

'Nothing is any fun without you, Alix,' he said pleadingly. 'You were my true love.'

'Or so I thought.' She disengaged her arm gently. 'Camilla is only one girl. Persevere and you'll finish up with somebody richer!'

Bitch, she thought on the way out, but it had been nice to say. In those terrible early months after their parents had been killed she could have done with Guy's support and comfort, but though Guy had valued her looks and personality he had valued her more as John Conroy's daughter. Thank God, he used to say, we'll have your father to build our house!

She had been blind, blind, blind, and tragedy had brought realisation.

When she arrived at the Ambassador she was in a sober, reflective mood, even spiritual.

'Alix, how lovely you look!' Richard Kaufmann was there to meet her, taking her arm and looking pleased and proud and protective. She looked like a lily tonight in her simple white dress and those pearls were superb. The feeling of being with a beautiful woman again warmed him to animation.

'What will we have to drink?' he asked, steering her into one of the discreetly opulent lounges.

If she was going to get through the night she thought she had better order something strong. 'A very dry Martini,' she smiled, wondering how he would react when he found out she was nothing but a gossip-hunter. Would he humiliate her in public? Would he grow angry, or would his only sign of distress be to call for another drink?

'I've been looking forward to this evening,' he said, his velvety brown eyes resting on her shining head. 'You have the most beautiful hair I think I've ever seen.'

'Then I'll never cut it, ever.'

He smiled, not wanting her to joke too much. For the first time in a very long time he felt at peace with himself and the world. Alix was very young, of course, but she had the makings of a fascinating woman. Not the sort of woman who had brought him to a decline and fall, but a ministering angel. There were many kinds of loving; many kinds of women.

Over their two pre-dinner drinks Alix introduced

topics she thought might be of interest to him, but she didn't attempt to bore him with politics. Politics would scarcely be of interest to a musician, and she was careful to steer off grand opera.

To her surprise, it was Richard who mentioned his famous ex-wife. 'I've heard from a close friend in New York that Adriana is considering a guest appearance at the Opera House.'

'But that's wonderful!' Alix, a concert goer, was genuinely excited.

'I can't say I share your joy,' Richard answered dryly.

'But she's a great artist, and we've never even seen her in this country.'

'I agree she's a great artist,' said Richard, evidently choosing his words, 'but the fact is I'm worried she'll take the opportunity to attack me.'

'But why would she do that?' Alix was much struck by the thought.

'In plain terms, Adriana is a bitch and she's incapable of keeping silent.'

'But I've never read a thing she's said about you.'

'Then I'll have to show you some of my cuttings,' Richard said with bitter humour. 'Don't you see, she's going to use this opportunity to describe me to the general public.'

'How awful!' Alix looked at him aghast, then when she saw his expression change, she added hastily, 'I mean, *would* it be awful?'

'Precisely.' Richard looked down at his drink. 'I just can't describe my life with Adriana. The force of her, the temperament! She took my ego and flattened it. Just as there are women who lift men to the skies, there are women who drag a man into hell.'

'You didn't create any difficulties yourself?' Alix asked gently.

'I believe I tried as much as I know how,' Richard answered simply. 'Shall we go into dinner?

'The stories I could tell you about Adriana would be too shocking to be true,' he said when they were settled in the velvet-upholstered banquette. 'What gives her the whip hand, of course, is she knows I'm a gentleman. Otherwise my retaliation would know no bounds.' As he was speaking, his strong long-fingered hand was resting lightly on hers.

'You must have loved her once,' Alix said, rather longing to draw her hand away.

'It has been truly said, my dear, that marriage is a battlefield, the partners more savage, more wicked, more motivated than opposing armies. I suppose I did love her at the beginning. Certainly I begged her to marry me. Up until then I'd led a charmed life.'

'So what caused you to fall out?'

'I didn't know what I was doing. I should never have married her in the first place. There's no creature on earth more jealous, more fierce, more insanely possessive than a lioness. What else could I do, I had to leave her before she destroyed me.'

'You're saying then Adriana's problem was psychological?' Alix asked. 'Jealousy without grounds?'

'Women have always been attracted to me,' Richard told her without vanity. 'I take no notice. I'm scarcely flattered. Sometimes, of course, depending on the woman, it can act as a stimulant. You've no idea how draining it is to be a performer. After a concert, there was usually a party to relax, and I must admit I thrive on a little female attention. Harmless stuff, but I couldn't convey that to Adriana in a way she found intelligible. I couldn't even look at another woman for more than three or four seconds. People used to hold their breath wondering what she was going to say—or do. The worst moment of my life was when she struck me in front of an entire audience.'

'And how did you respond?' Alix looked back at him, dismayed.

'Actually, for the one and only time in my life, I struck a woman back. I don't think I've had one happy minute since.'

'If you take that a step further,' Alix prompted 'couldn't it mean you still care about her? That you regret your action?'

The waiter, who had been hovering, sensed a gap in the conversation and capitalised on it. Richard had been recognised by now and people had started to turn heads, careless of the futile, cautionary words: Don't look now. Everyone knew it was Richard Kaufmann the concert pianist, but no one could seem to place Alix. All were in agreement, however, that she was a lovely-looking young woman and at least fifteen years too young for her companion.

Richard chose the menu with care, deferring only slightly to Alix. It was obvious he had a burning need to be a mentor, and Alix could understand this after his recent tempestuous relationship with a woman who apparently had dominated him to death. At least he was an expert, and in any case she was more fascinated with the talk.

For good measure, after the wine waiter had gone, he told her a few more of his great moments with

Adriana, until Alix began to suspect he was playing a game with her. Did he know she was a reporter after all? If so, he wasn't unhappy about it, rather, impelled to talk. The words simply flowed from him like possibly his favourite piece.

'Well, I never!' said Alix when he briefly paused.

'Ah, women!' He gave her an ironic, worldly smile. 'I must stop right here, however. Secrets in marriage should be treated like the confessional.' He looked stunningly handsome, faintly decadent, with his full mouth twisted in a wry grimace.

'Why, hi there!' a voice said behind Alix, and a hand slipped on to her shoulder.

Shocked and revolted, Alix looked up quickly at her old office chum. She couldn't cut her, but somehow she would have to get rid of her. Of all the rotten tricks!

'Oh, how are you, Val,' she said offhandedly, and inclined her head at Val's happily innocent companion.

'Aren't you the clever one!' Val said archly, and transferred her amber gaze to Richard Kaufmann's totally expressionless face. 'Who'd ever believe you'd get an interview with the great Richard Kaufmann? I'm Val Turner, by the way,' she introduced herself to the great man. 'My friend Tony Meagher. . . .'

'Don't we have to go?' Tony interrupted, looking at Alix's embarrassed, angry face.

'Never. Why?' Val gave a very odd laugh. '*Impact* is going to be pretty happy with Richard Kaufmann on the cover.'

'I take it you're a reporter too,' Richard Kaufmann asked suddenly, his accent stunningly frigid and plummy.

'More or less.' Val smiled. 'I don't get the pick of the interviews like Alix here, but I'm good at my job.'

'What job?' Alix looked at her with disgust.

'There are other magazines besides *Impact*.'

'Just so long as they don't mind the kind of thing you do.'

'I'm sure you're right!' Richard Kaufmann said, and looked pointedly at Val's by now awkward companion.

'Excuse us, won't you?' said Tony Meagher, and drew Val determinedly away out of delicacy.

'So there we are!' said Alix. Not that she hadn't learned a great deal.

'What a ghastly young woman,' Richard answered, relieved she had gone.

'And no friend of mine.' Alix hung her shining head. 'How long have you known I'm a journalist?'

Richard smiled and patted her hand. 'I would never have known, only I happened to pick up your magazine. The girl on the cover looked extraordinarily like Adriana when she was young. Italian, of course. There's hardly an Italian girl who isn't beautiful.'

'And you're not angry?' Alix looked at him with shimmering eyes. 'You have every right to be.'

'I don't think you understand, Alix,' he said dryly.' People have been running after me for years. When one reaches the top and one has a certain aura one is perpetually in demand. Not so much here, perhaps, which is one reason I came home, but in America I've been immensely successful on television. Adriana, too. She comes over like a cross between the great Callas and Sophia Loren. I've been conned into giving interviews time and time again, so I'm not going to be too angry with you. At least you do it all very nicely.'

'It's my job,' said Alix, willing him to understand. 'I would have much preferred to ring and make an appointment for an interview, but we all know you've been determinedly incommunicado.'

'Waiting for my wounds to heal,' Richard explained. 'You know how it is, musicians are a sensitive lot.'

'Yes!' Alix seized on the word. Richard clearly saw himself as the extremely hyper-sensitive variety. 'I couldn't have been asked to do an interview I would have wanted to do more, only it worried me dreadfully to violate your privacy. Did you know that?'

Richard nodded his dark head. 'If you weren't such a sensitive girl you wouldn't manage such good interviews. The one you did with Lewis Wollcott, for example. I liked that very much. I'm sure he liked it too.'

'Yes, he did.' The waiter approached to refill Alix's wine glass. 'Actually he told me people had become a whole lot more interested in his work because of our coverage. We presented him as a real person, not a boring old classical music composer. People's ideas are changing a lot. The better informed they become, the wider their interests.'

'And you want to do a sketch of my life's work?' Richard raised his brown eyes to look into hers.

'You represent one of our great national heroes. Great concert pianists aren't born every day, neither are they devastatingly handsome. So far as your private life goes, you can say as much or as little as you like. Naturally, the public are interested in as much as you'll tell them. We would like you to appear on our cover. I'm sure you're very well aware you're extremely photogenic.'

'I am,' said Richard and made way for the superb Sydney rock oysters. 'Besides, it's time I opened up a little. Artists of my level can't continue to live in a glass case. Besides, it would put Adriana's nose out of joint. . . .'

'Besides,' Alix said interrupting, 'if you think she's going to talk about you, mightn't it be as well to present *your* angle? Without shocking anyone, of course.'

'Perhaps we'd better wait until you've got your tape recorder,' Richard pointed out quite pleasantly, and drew her attention to the excellence of the oysters.

CHAPTER SIX

THE Christmas edition of *Impact* proved to be a sell-out. Better, it earned Alix a nice bonus and a real place as an interviewer. The cover shot was brilliant; a little corny to the magazines that had missed out but visually so romantic—Chopinesque, with Richard poised over the keys of a magnificent concert grand, he sold more records in the following weeks than he had done in a year. Moreover, he had now successfully established himself as Alix's friend and mentor; a purely platonic arrangement, because that was how Alix definitely wanted it, but mutually pleasurable and rewarding.

'And just how long do you think that state of affairs is going to go on?' Carl asked her at the office party.

'I'm wondering why you want to know?' The little smile she gave him was more a reflex action than any indication of friendliness.

'God, Conroy,' he said dryly,' from what I've read about Crespi, she just could fire a shot into you.'

'What nonsense!' Her creamy white skin faintly blanched. 'She has nothing whatever to do with him now.'

'Child,' he said jeeringly, 'what do you suppose is really bringing her to Australia? She's on record as saying she detests travelling. It's a long way.'

'Then call it a desire to conquer a whole new continent,' she said tartly. Whatever had persuaded him

to invite Barbra Gould to the office party? Alix eyed
her over Carl's head. She looked stunning in black
and white, laughing at something Gary was saying to
her. It was exactly as though he wanted to tell her
their dangerous moment was past. Now why the devil
should that hurt?

Barbra came over, drawling a hello, but her dark
eyes were flat as they rested directly on Alix's face.

'This is a delightful party, I don't really want to
go.'

'Then stay for a long time,' Alix suggested sweetly.
Did Barbra think she was blind? There was dislike in
those flat dark eyes. Dislike and a warning: *Leave my
man alone.*

'I'd like to,' Barbra answered, without hesitation,
'but I'm looking out a few things for Carl!' Again that
challenging, flat-eyed smile.

'Furnishings?' Alix enquired politely.

'Oh, yes. Some antique, some modern. He's only
taking a few things out of the apartment.'

'Really?' Alix felt a rush of fright and pain. If he
was leaving the apartment, that must mean he was
shifting in elsewhere.

'We're hoping to do most of his decorating,' Barbra
said rather aggressively. 'It's a wonderful house.
Wonderful!'

'You've seen over it?' Alix thought she was going to
faint.

'Yes, of course.' Barbra's shiny dark eyes looked
nastier than ever. 'I'm aware it was your family
home. You looked shocked.'

'For one thing, that he could afford the price,' Alix
said tartly.

'But he's far from being a poor man.' Barbra looked back at her, faintly surprised. 'Surely you remember reading or hearing that old Daniel Mellish left him a tidy sum? It wasn't all that long ago. Apparently the old boy thought the world of Carl. Some even went so far as to say he just could have been Carl's father. Don't forget he was an orphan.'

'Who knows?' Alix shrugged her shoulders as though she couldn't care less. She mustn't, *mustn't* cry or she would drown in her own tears. Carl Danning and this woman in her father's house?

'Of course I can understand your missing such a splendid environment,' Barbra said kindly. 'In many ways your father had a heroic style and the house is so wonderfully integrated with its site. Carl didn't favour us much with his apartment, but we're hoping for better things with the house. He's so busy for so much of the time and it's such a big job. I'm confident he'll come to realise he'll need help.'

'No doubt about that!' Alix tried desperately for a smile and swept up from her seat. 'His own apartment would fit neatly in the laundry.'

As she brusquely took her departure, she knocked a paperweight from the desk, but she didn't even turn around to retrieve it. Where did Barbra Gould get her information from? Carl Danning Daniel Mellish's son? It didn't seem in the least likely, though even the most highly regarded public figures had been known to lead double lives. Not Sir Daniel, she felt sure. A man like that, with a long distinguished record at the Bar, would have found a much better way to take care of that kind of a situation. Carl Danning, on his own admission, had had a hard life, but even that and his prodigious drive and intelligence, moreover, his arrogance, didn't entitle him to aspire to own the house their father had called his finest, most reward- ing achievement.

People seemed to be calling everywhere, but Alix kept on walking. When the party broke up they were all free to go home. She was just going home a little earlier.

'*Alix!*'

Something in his tone stopped her, an adamancy and a determination.

'You could perfectly well have said goodbye.'

'Goodbye,' she said curtly. 'You'll have to excuse me, but I'm dying with envy.'

'Would it make you happy if someone else moved into your home?' He came towards her, looking every inch the tough guy she supposed him to be.

She hated him so much she could kill him, but she wouldn't let him see. 'I think we can all agree I'm not being rational about this.'

His blunt-featured, formidable dark face was equally intense. 'There are some things, Alix, one is destined to have.'

'According to you,' she nearly shouted, 'John Conroy's house. The house he built with love, for his family.' Suddenly it all came back, the halcyon days of her childhood, her teens which were never difficult at all, but wonderfully happy and secure. Her eyes were blinded with tears. She couldn't think or speak or even act calmly.

'I'll *give* it to you,' he said in a wretched voice, and began to draw her shaking body towards him. 'Live with me and it's yours!'

Her smoky eyes went blank with shock and she had to suck in her breath. She didn't want to hear him speak such wanton, lustful craziness.

'Alix,' he said, and though she held her body rigid, his hand rubbing up and down her back made her body relax. Somehow she was resting against him and his hand was in her hair.

'How horrible you are!' she said feelingly. 'You're making it so I have to get away from you.'

'You can't.' The action that had started out as a blind impulse to comfort was turning into something else.

'Carl?'

It was a woman's voice and both of them recognised it immediately. 'Let me go!' Alix exclaimed violently, horrified at the thought of being caught in his arms.

'Don't cry, Alix. *Please* don't.'

'I'm not crying!' She choked back a pitiful sob, positively unnerved by the treacherous cadences in his deep voice. 'There's one thing I *do* know, Barbra Gould will make a mess of the decorating. She's never even *been* in a house like ours.'

'I just happened to catch that,' Barbra called out, affronted, from the stairs. 'Let me tell you, Miss Conroy. . . .'

'I wish you wouldn't!' Carl said wearily, turning his thickly thatched dark head.

'If you say so, Carl.' Instantly Barbra came to heel. 'Really, I'm very sorry for Miss Conroy. It must be difficult.'

It was more than difficult, Alix thought, rushing headlong away from them. So churned up was she inside, she very nearly had an accident on the way home. Normally a competent and considerate driver, when an insufferable young idiot in a panel van tried to cut in on her, instead of giving way in the interests of safety, she stood on the accelerator and risked a neck-and-neck collision.

Afterwards, she looked at herself aghast and saw tears trickling down her cheeks. Part of her sadness and loss of serenity was the fact that it was Christmas. It was such a very special time; a time to be with one's loved ones, one's family, close friends. She would never, *ever*, get over the tragic death of her parents. Indeed it often seemed to her they were only away on holiday and must surely come back.

Peter had found himself a job at the local supermarket for a few weeks of the school vacation, so she had to wait a few hours until he arrived home.

He came in smiling with pleasure, exulting over his pay. 'If I keep this up, I'll be a millionaire!' A little clumsily he grabbed and hugged her, and Alix had to throw an arm around him to save herself from falling over.

'What's happening around here? One day you're my little brother, now you can throw me around like a box of groceries!'

'Which reminds me,' he walked to the refrigerator and opened it, 'you didn't happen to buy chocolate icecream?'

'No, I didn't!' she said jerkily.

'Why, what's the matter?' Peter looked back at her with surprised concern.

'Oh, nothing!' She tried to smile so he wouldn't see she was unhappy.

'Come on, *give*.' It was her father's face looking at her, calm and strong.

'It's the house!' she said despairingly, and burst into tears.

'Our house?' Peter grasped her arm firmly and led her back into the sitting room.

'Yes,' she said, dashing the tears away with the back of her hand.

'And it's breaking your heart.'

'Yes.' Alix hung her blonde head.

'You didn't break down when we had to sell out to the McNeills.'

'It seemed so necessary then.'

'Then I suppose it's Carl,' said Peter, coming right to the heart of the matter.

'I'd rather let it go to anyone but him,' Alix told him in a quiet, pathetic voice.

'Even if he's going to love it and look after it and bring the whole place alive. He's that kind of a man, you know—vibrant, like Dad.'

'He's nothing like Daddy!' Alix cried, aghast and emotional.

'For some mysterious reason,' Peter persisted, 'I think he is.'

'Because you admire him.'

'I do. He's not as gentlemanly as Dad, I mean as smooth or refined or something, but he's got the same kind of mind; brilliant and quick and aware. More, if you notice he really takes notice of kids. He's kind. He even goes back to that old orphanage.'

'Does he really?' Alix lifted her head in surprise. 'You seem to know an awful lot about him.'

'He talks to me, that's why. You won't let him. I

think you're frightened of him, myself. As a matter of fact you told me you loathed him at your very first meeting.'

'Have we ever discussed the possibility of your studying psychiatry?' Alix suddenly smiled.

'You know what I intend to do,' Peter laid a tender hand on her head. 'I'm going to be an architect, like Dad. Don't worry about the house. Some day I'll build you, not a better one, but maybe just as good.'

'You're beautiful,' Alix told him, trying to stop her mouth trembling. 'What say we go out for tea?'

'Do you think you could suffer McDonald's?' Peter asked hopefully. Not for him haute cuisine but Big Mac hamburgers and the like.

'Why don't you ring Rusty?' asked Alix. 'As I recall, he's pretty big on double malts.'

'Right!' Peter grinned at her and went to do what he was told.

Who wouldn't love a brother like that? Alix thought. It was just as well she wasn't hungry.

Over the boy's second Big Mac, Rusty confided his parents had rented a beach house on Queensland's Gold Coast for most of the school vacation.

'Lucky you!' Alix smiled at him with real affection. The boys had been friends for so long Rusty was almost family. 'Whereabouts on the Coast?'

'Not Surfers Paradise, it's too busy there. Mum and Dad like it quiet. We're going to a little spot called Tugun. The house is right on the beach. Mum's going to ring you.'

'Rusty wants me to go,' Peter explained quickly, 'but I told him no.'

'But, darling, of course you can go!' Alix looked at

her brother's suddenly worried face. 'You'll have a lovely time. It's so kind of Rusty's parents to ask you.'

'No,' Peter said firmly. 'I'm staying home to take care of you.'

'That's what he said,' Rusty nodded his flaming head. 'When I told Mum, she said: "It just goes to show what a fine boy you have for a friend!" '

'Oh, shut up,' Peter muttered.

'Anyway, Mum's going to ring,' Rusty finished off his french fries. 'She said she'll be able to work out something with Alix.'

'Good.' Alix smiled at him and asked Peter to get her another cup of coffee. Even before their parents had died, Peter had always been allowed to spend at least a week of the long summer vacation with Rusty and his family. She knew she wouldn't be able to get him to leave her over the Christmas/New Year holiday, neither could she bear to part with him, but a holiday on the Gold Coast would do him the world of good. She had already begun to worry about his staying around the unit when his job ran out, and this year she couldn't manage Christmas leave.

When she dropped Rusty off, Helen Maclean came out to the car. 'Well, how did it go?'

'*Beaut!*' Rusty thanked Alix again and jumped out. 'I told Alix about going to the Coast.'

'Oh, dear, Rusty!' Helen's round, pretty face looked perturbed. 'Didn't I tell you *I* was going to speak to Alix?'

'Sure, Mum,' Rusty put his arm around his mother's waist. 'Tell her now.'

'Won't you come in, Alix?' Helen invited. 'James isn't home yet, but I'm expecting him shortly. Of course we want Peter to come with us, but naturally I was going to discuss it first with you.'

'I can't think of anything nicer for Peter's vacation,' Alix smiled at the older woman, following her in. 'You've always been so kind to him, Helen. You and James.'

'That's not difficult,' Helen looked back at the whispering boys. 'He's an exceptional boy. I hope they'll always be the greatest of friends.'

A week later, Alix put Peter on a northbound plane and returned to the empty unit. It was inevitable she would be lonely, but she placed Peter's needs far above her own. He had worked hard all year; his end-of-term report had been straight sevens, so he deserved a complete break and the companionship of a boy his own age.

Still, she was lonely.

'What's the matter?' Gary asked her one day.

'I'm sorry.' She set down her pen and swivelled round to look at him. 'I'm not very good company.'

'Missing Pete, no doubt.'

'Yes, I am.'

'Then I've definitely decided we're going to give a party, Marj and I. Don't come if you don't want.'

'When?' She smiled into his kindly, humorous blue eyes.

'What about Saturday night? Marj and I could do with a bit of fun. Sometimes I think I can scarcely remember what it was like. The kids can go over to her mum's. They'll come back spoilt as hell, but we won't worry about that.'

'Actually I'm having dinner with Richard,' she suddenly remembered, looking disappointed.

'Bring 'im!'

'Okay!' Her grey eyes lit up. 'What can I do to help?'

'Just leave it, miss, to me. Marj will take care of it.'

Richard seemed very surprised and hesitant when Alix suggested they go to a colleague's party, but in the end he consented. Public response and the boom in the sale of his records had considerably sweetened his melancholia and he was becoming genuinely fond of Alix. Marriage with Adriana had choked him, now he was feeling free.

By the time they arrived at the Pearsons' pleasant suburban home, the party was well in progress. People stood round laughing and talking and some were dancing on the pergola-covered patio.

'I'm glad you could come, Mr Kaufmann,' Gary gave the older man a welcoming smile. 'We do have a piano, but no one is going to ask you to do anything you don't want.'

'We've brought you a little gift,' Richard smiled equally pleasantly, and put a bottle of wine into Gary's hand.

'You didn't have to do this.'

'We wanted to.' Alix patted his arm. 'Where's Marj?'

'In the kitchen. I wouldn't go in there if I were you. The last time I looked in she was waving a knife.'

'Hi!' Alix smiled over Gary's shoulder and jiggled her fingers in greeting. All of the office were there so far as she could see, but mercifully not Carl Danning.

At least a dozen strange faces.

'Come and I'll introduce you around,' Gary said, beaming. 'That's some dress, Alix. You look terrific!'

Less than an hour later, when she was having a thoroughly good time and Richard had begun to relax, Carl Danning arrived.

For some extraordinary reason, Alix couldn't tear her eyes off him. In an over-populated world, he was one of those rare beings who carried an actual aura of burning vitality. It was like being surrounded by one's own magnetic field, readily perceived by the naked eye. Her father, too, had carried his radiance into a room, and Alix saw bleakly what Peter had meant. In their different ways, both men belonged to a select band.

When he glanced briefly in her direction with his black eyes, he must have caught her expression, for his transforming smile faded.

'Someone has asked me to play,' Richard told her, surprisingly out of the side of his mouth.

'How lovely for all of us.'

'Oh, God, I don't want to. I *can't*!'

'That's not true, Richard.' She spoke to him exactly as she might have spoken to Peter.

'You can't know.' He looked down at his strong, clenched hands. 'Adriana robbed me of everything, even my talent.'

'You mean she put a hex on you? Or put it another way, pointed the bone? I thought you were far too intelligent for that!'

'Whatever it was,' Richard's handsome face turned vulnerable, 'it's worked!'

'Now, now, that's nonsense!' Despite herself, Alix

was caught up in his fears. She put her slender, taper-
ing hand over his and gripped tight. 'You mustn't
wait for Adriana to free you. You must free yourself.'
She suddenly jumped up, startling him.

'Can we have a little quiet?'

'*Alix!*' Richard's anguished whisper reached her.

For a moment she thought she would burst into
tears on his account, but she had to shock him into
action.

'Richard has very kindly consented to play for us.'

'Oh, splendid . . . bravo!'

There was not an instant's hesitation from anybody, and a burst of clapping rang out.

It was Carl who went to the almost new upright
piano, bought for the children to learn on, removed
the flowers and opened up the lid.

Richard got to his feet almost glassy-eyed, then as
though magnetised by the other man's intense stare
walked towards him, standing compellingly by the
piano. They shook hands and Carl said something
that made Richard's pale face crease into a smile of
ironic amusement. He shrugged and responded to
Carl's quick, enquiring glance. Carl had been good
with Richard, right from the beginning; he had
even enticed him down to the office, got him to talk
even more. A natural-born leader and confidant.
Alix wondered why she should be so constantly surprised.

As soon as Richard settled himself on the seat, Carl
walked across to where Alix was sitting, obviously
expecting her to move a little so he could join her on
the sofa.

She gave him a quick, troubled smile, taking note

of the way her body trembled when confronted by the nearness of his.

'Thank you, Alix,' he said dryly, as though nothing she thought was any great secret to him.

Richard continued to stare frowningly at the keys with such concentration Marj began to think he was offended at having to play such an inferior instrument. She even went to rise, but Gary caught her hand. No matter how long it took, Kaufmann had to play.

No one dared clear their throat, though it was apparent they would have to wait for the great man to impart his party piece. Some were already starting to feel anxious. All of them had read Alix's telling interview.

Alix too was feeling deep misgivings. *She* had forced Richard into this. Maybe he *had* lost his powers.

The whole situation was fraught with risk.

She closed her eyes and set her mind to pray, trembling violently when Carl took her hand in his. Such warm hands, square and confident. No woman would emasculate Carl. This she knew from the very depths of her being.

'So the canary won't sing!' he said softly in her ear.

'Oh, God!' She opened her eyes and looked at him for a wordless minute.

Richard was still glowering at the keys, his dark head turned slightly to one side, the large living room silent and quizzical, when suddenly Carl called in his beautiful, vibrant voice.

'May I be selfish, Richard, and ask for a request?'

The sound of a human voice appeared to jolt Richard to life. He turned his head and looked at the other man as though he wasn't totally abandoned.

'Yes, Carl?'

'I heard you play at a festival in New York. After the concerto you were brought back so many times, you played an encore. I don't remember the name of the piece, but I remember how it goes. If you'll excuse me. . . .' Carl got up and walked to the piano, leaning over it as Richard shifted to one side. 'Terrific piece. I've always remembered it. Went something like this. . . .' He found a note in the bass with his big hand and began hammering it rhythmically, moving to a chord.

'The Mephisto Waltz, of course!' Richard said in a clipped professional tone, wincing a little as Carl hammered away determinedly. 'It's from Lenau's *Faust*.'

'That's the one!' Carl moved off happily, and, no doubt thinking he could scarcely do worse, Richard broke into the brilliant and extremely difficult waltz.

'My God!' Marj whispered to her husband. She had never thought to hear her piano sounding so good.

As though driven by the devil himself, Richard took it at a dazzling presto. He was superb, the left hand, the right hand, the scintillating runs. When he finally brought the bravura piece to a close, the silence was electric and those neighbours of the Pearsons who hadn't been invited were sitting out in semicircles on their front stairs.

From then on, he played anything and everything; some stunningly good jazz. A very pretty girl who had accompanied Gary's young brother sat down on the long piano seat beside him and started to croon. He said something to her and she smiled and nodded, then began to sing. It was one of Cleo Laine's numbers and she put it across very well, Richard backing her with considerable panache. It was evident he was happy and relaxed, and, much relieved, Alix moved out on to the patio.

'Come looking for me?' a familiar voice said, and Carl took her hand.

'*Thanks*,' she said feelingly.

'What for?' he turned her towards him, looking at her hair and her skin and her flowered red crêpe-de-chine strapless dress.

'For helping Richard.'

'But then he needs help.'

'So do most of us.'

'What have we now?' he asked dryly. 'An act of martyrdom? Believe me, Conroy, you wouldn't know how to cope with our Richard. You think you understand him, but you don't. My advice remains. Keep him at a safe distance.'

'Only you have the right to get any closer, is that it?'

'Physically, Conroy, I found you intoxicating, but. . . .'

'Where's Barbra?' she said sweetly. 'May I ask the question?'

'There's a limit to the number of times I see the same woman in the one week.' He took her arm and led her away across the lawn. 'They've got a very nice little place here. Gary's done a lot, the decking, the retaining wall, now he wants to put a pool in for the kids. He's got room and that natural depression will save a lot of excavating.'

'You're not proposing we tour around in the dark?' Alix meant to sound cool, continue their everlasting skirmish with words, but his hand over hers ensured his domination. Instant possession; a force so strong she couldn't refuse it.

'How's Peter?' He didn't answer her, looking up at the blossoming stars.

'He's fine.' Her voice was shaky now and soft with fright. 'I get a postcard every other day.'

'You're very close, aren't you?'

'We always were. Even before . . . even. . . .'

'Yes.' His grip tightened on her hand. 'You'll have to be careful to marry the right man, someone who's going to love and appreciate Peter. The gossips have been whispering behind your back that you're seeing your ex-fiancé.'

'When have you ever wanted to listen to gossip?'

'All the time.' His clearly delineated mouth curved slightly. 'Don't you see, Alix, he can't just pick you up and put you down.'

'You *believe* I'm seeing him,' she said angrily, and pulled against his hand to stop.

'I believe he's been present outside our building every afternoon last week.'

'A lot of men can't accept defeat.'

'Would you like me to handle it?' he asked blandly.

'What would you say?' She looked up at his dark face, feeling she was whirling in space.

'Alix belongs to me.'

She couldn't judge from his voice whether he was fooling or not, but his words hit her so hard she thought she was going to stutter.

'You m-mean if you told him a lie, you think he'd go away?'

'It's worth a try.' He put a hand under her smooth silky hair and cupped her nape. 'I'm going to have to kiss you soon, Conroy, or I'll go mad.'

'You don't seem to like the idea!' She held her head back challenging him.

'I love it!' He drew her closer. 'I mean, if I don't think about things.'

'What's the sense to it all, then?'

'I like your dress.' He brought his other hand up over her breast, and curiously that confident hand trembled.

'We'll be missed!' She drove herself to tell him. In another minute she wouldn't be able to think at all.

'All right,' he sighed deeply. 'We'll wait until later. I even dream about making love to you.'

'So you figure once I'm out of your system you'll get a restful night?' Perversely, because he had let her go, she was angry.

'Not another reason why!' He laughed. 'You look like an angel, Alix, but I'm not about to saddle myself with a hot-tempered woman. The excitement now is stopping your mouth, but think what a time you'd give me!'

They didn't leave the party until after two, and Richard drove her home, laughing and talking and wide awake.

'I can't remember when I had such a tremendous

night!' he said enthusiastically. 'Such nice people, so friendly and unassuming.'

'You were the undoubted star of the evening!' Alix looked kindly at his animated profile. 'A night to remember.'

'For the whole neighbourhood, I believe. Marj told me all the neighbours were out on the street.'

'It's not every day one can get to hear the great Richard Kaufmann, for nothing and in their own back yard!'

'Thank you, Alix,' he said softly, and stole a look at her. 'You've worked your own spell, you know. There was a time I thought my wounds would never heal, but you've helped me back to life. You and Carl. You know, I heard his voice from a distance. I was utterly bemused, but there's something about the man, some power. It's impossible to explain. My old professor had it in abundance. Certain people can make things happen. Of course the joke is, I believe he plays quite well.'

'*Carl* does?' Alix could do no more than stare at him.

'So Gary was saying. He was out there one day and played for the kids. He had no formal training except for a brief period when he was adopted, but apparently he used to bash away at the old piano at the orphanage. One of the nuns used to try and help him. An extraordinary man, naturally gifted.'

'Apparently.' Alix's voice was faint and she had a sudden vision of a sturdy little boy with an unruly mop of black hair and black eyes working out his pain and frustrations on the yellowing keys of an old piano.

'When Adriana comes,' Richard said fervently, 'I believe I can face her.'

'Why not?' Especially in a city this size, she thought ironically. Plenty of places to run and hide.

'How about us all going to lunch one day next week?' Richard suggested happily. 'You and me and Gary and Carl? Marj won't be able to leave the children, but I'll think of something for her. I'm buying, of course.'

'Sounds nice!' Alix encouraged him. The stronger Richard felt, the more surrounded by friends, the more easily he would be able to confront the woman who had torn his life, his career, his confidence to shreds.

Or *had* she? Despite the wealth of evidence Richard had supplied to the contrary, Alix had a sneaking fellow feeling for Adriana. Such a brilliant artist couldn't be totally bad. Older than Richard, with her dramatic beauty slavishly maintained, she would have her moments of insecurity. Richard, on his own admission, was a connoisseur of a woman's charms. Who could help but understand Adriana's passionate surges of jealousy? She might even be a very nice person.

'May I come up?' Richard asked as they approached the lift.

'I am rather tired,' Alix smiled at him very sweetly, keeping her expression trusting.

'Of course you are!' He glanced swiftly at his superb gold watch. 'I'll ring you tomorrow.' He put his hands on her shoulders and kissed her softly and gently on the mouth. 'God bless!'

He saw her into the lift and she waved him off.

Dear Richard! She had developed quite a protective instinct towards him. Still, you couldn't put the lot down to Adriana.

Head bent, searching out her keys, she didn't see the tall, powerfully built man lounging by her door.

'Remember me?'

His voice shocked her, so much so that she put a hand to her mouth to choke back a scream.

'How dare you come here, *frighten* me!' she snapped wrathfully.

'I always keep my promises.'

The expression on his face made the keys fall out of her nerveless hands. Black eyes glinted. Powerful shoulders faintly hunching like the heavyweight champion about to lash out. She felt pitifully small and defenceless, so to compensate she hit out with her tongue.

'You're not spending the night *here*!'

He took a deep breath as though he was trying to control himself. 'Never. You'll have to fight to keep me in.'

'Then why come by?'

'I told you,' he bent swiftly and retrieved her keys, 'I've got it all arranged to kiss you tonight.' He grabbed her hand tightly, pulled her to him, and inserted the key in the door. 'Quiet now, you don't want to wake the neighbours.'

Alix flushed violently, realising she was trembling from head to toe. 'I *won't* let this happen!'

'You've already done so.' He drew her inside the dark of the hall where there wasn't even a spark of light, leaned against the closed door and pulled her slender fragile body to his.

She had expected some violence, a breathless reign of terror, but his tenderness seduced her completely.

He's a demon, she told herself. A demon. He knowns exactly what I like and want.

His kisses on her open, upturned mouth were sweeter than anything she could have imagined. Sweeter again than that other time. Without her even knowing it, her arms had encircled him and she was pressing herself ever closer to his curiously yearning hard male body.

Was it her heart or his that beat so loudly?

After a while he picked her up, his eyes cat-like in the dark.

I think I love you, Alix thought. How can I? She was incapable of coherent thought.

In her bedroom, Carl put her down gently on the bed and she slumped right over on her side and hid her face beneath the heavy fall of her hair.

Tell him you're a virgin.

He knows.

Tell him everything. Your hopes and your fears.

'Easy, darling,' he said, and drew her back against him.

He had removed his jacket and she felt the smooth fabric of his shirt against her cheek. It smelled clean and fresh. Like him. Spiked with the scent of his after-shave cologne.

'Alix, are you all right?' He got his hand beneath her chin.

Don't ask me, she thought. Don't ask me. I'm a woman at war with my own set of rules. The infinite tenderness of his lovemaking had defeated her utterly. If he had sought to overcome her by force, he would never have got the best of her. As it was, they were here together on her bed.

'You're so lovely!' he muttered, his voice low and husky. 'I want you so much. *God!*' He sounded as if he was having a titan struggle with himself.

Alix tilted her head right back on his shoulder and his hands came up under her breasts and lifted them, his thumbs gently stroking the nipples so they sprang into erotic life.

'Are dreams dangerous, Alix?' he whispered, and when she didn't answer he lowered his mouth to hers again, kissing her so deeply they both fell together on to the pillows.

There must have been tears on her cheeks again, because she heard him say, 'Alix, it's all right!' his hand smoothing her back as if she were a baby.

Somehow her breasts were pressed against his naked chest and his breathing had become deep and ragged.

'You're a virgin, aren't you?' He pressed his mouth to the delicate hollow at the base of her throat.

'Yes.' Her chin came down on his thick, springy hair. It was wonderful hair. Hair to get your fingers into and pull.

'Would it kill you to have my child?' His mouth moved over her breast.

'I don't *know* you, Carl. I don't know you at all!'

So why was she holding him closer, ever closer?

'For better or worse, we're together. You're my woman.'

'*No!*'

'Would you let anyone else touch you like this? Here . . . and here?' His voice sank to a whisper.

It would be easy, so easy to believe he really cared. She wanted him so much, she could have cried aloud with it, but her instinct for self-preservation was very strong. Hers was not the temperament for affairs. She wanted a beautiful marriage like her parents had had; sacred and holy, each totally committed to the other, the new life they had brought into the world. To Alix, sex was love, and love meant a deep, mutual caring. Caring about the afterwards, not the now.

'Why do you want a child?' she whispered, her hands tender on his heavy dark head.

'I want a family!' He turned his head into the cool, scented valley between her breasts. 'I want to give them everything I never got—a mother like an angel, peace, security, a big house to have fun in. Almost every night I think about the kids I haven't got.'

'You're a strange man,' she said softly. 'A mystery.'

'That's because you won't let me talk to you.' He lifted his head to look into her face. 'You've never wanted to talk to me. In fact, I've felt your dislike pretty strongly.'

'We're here now,' she pointed out with some bewilderment.

'And it's wonderful. Very. But I want a great deal more from you.'

'Please, Carl, don't say any more.' His intensity frightened her. The thought of being swamped by his powerful personality.

'There's something about me you find oppressive,' he said broodingly. 'I realise this, but I *can't* act lightly, lightheartedly, whatever. It's not me. In a lot of ways my life has been savage. It's what turned me into a winner. I want to win everything. I want to win *you*.'

'Because you think I'm unattainable?'

'You're *not* for me,' he kissed her trembling mouth.

'Do you love me?' she questioned him, when her heart beat had settled.

'What do you think?' He leaned over and switched on the bedside lamp so it bathed them in a golden glow.

'I think you've never learned how to love.' She put a hand down to cover her naked breasts, but he moved her hand away.

'What does that matter!' Determination rang in his dark, vibrant voice, showed itself plainly in the firm set of his mouth and jawline. 'If you give me your word one day you'll marry me, I'll go home.'

'*No!*' The shock made her move her head fretfully from side to side.

'You're beautiful, Alix. So very beautiful.' His strong hands cupped her head and held it still. 'You think I know everything about women. I know a lot that doesn't really matter. I never had a mother or a sister. The nuns in the orphanage were good women, kind and dedicated, but they, too, were trained to hide their feelings. Tenderness, love, as you knew it, was very nearly forbidden. I'm still human enough to want you. And Peter.'

'Please, Carl,' she said pleadingly, 'you won't even let me catch my breath. How could I possibly know you were thinking all this?'

'You mean you never had an inkling in all this time?' His black eyes glittered.

'I knew you were attracted to me, that's all.' His beautiful shirt was open to the waist and she could see his powerful chest and rib cage, the matting of dark hair. He was in superb physical condition, hard and taut. Probably every fight he had ever had as a small boy he had won. Alix's emotions were veering wildly all over the place. Now she was filled with an over-whelming tenderness, and, seeing her face, Carl arched her to him, wrapping his arms around her so tightly it seemed she would never get away.

'I'll have you one way or the other. What's it to be, marriage?'

'This is blackmail!'

'Yes.' He pressed his mouth to her throat. 'I'm short on the virtues.'

'The last thing I want to do is get married.' The truth was, she wanted *him* without marriage.

'You can't keep Peter cooped up in this damned unit any longer. He deserves more.'

It was the most telling approach he could have used, and he was a clever man. 'What would you want of me?' Alix sighed deeply as though all the fight had gone out of her.

'Your sacred vows, permanent and binding. No divorce with me, Alix. No broken family. No broken home.'

'I think I'm trying to say you expect me to sleep with you?'

'Wouldn't you be interested?' He gave her a long, revealing look.

'I have to think!' She tried to get her hand up to put it to her face. It was almost like being drowned.

She couldn't even get a hand above water.

'Between the two of us,' he said dryly, 'I think you'll say yes.' He moved her gently back on to the bed and stood up, drinking in the sight of her, the slender body and luminous skin.

'If only you'd say you *care* for me!' She sat up abruptly, gold hair spilling wildly.

'Of course I care!' His mouth twisted wryly. 'I care enough to give you a couple of days.'

She was conscious then of the inevitability of it all, the way fate had delivered her into his hands. She was vaguely aware she should make some kind of protest, some declaration of self, but she was too tired, too spent with emotion. She had always thought of their relationship as a contest, now she was beaten to her knees.

Such a strange man! Complex.

Aware of his intent gaze, she lifted her hand and pushed back her tumbled hair. The action lifted her breasts and she heard him draw in his breath sharply.

'Do you really think I could let you go now?' he asked. 'If I even get out this door it will be a miracle.'

'You promised.' She pulled herself to her feet, silky strands of her hair clinging to her shoulders and her flushed cheeks.

For a moment Carl didn't move or speak, then he walked towards the door. 'Just to clear up any confusion, you might tell Kaufmann. He must surely know in any case, he's old enough to be your father.'

'Richard doesn't love me one little bit,' she called after him urgently.

'Just as well.' His own thoughts made him narrow his eyes. 'By the way, you might as well be the first to know, I'm quitting the magazine. I'm going into politics.'

'What?' *What?* she thought dazedly. If anyone could make Prime Minister, he could.

'High time you knew,' he said, and gave her a brilliant look. 'If anyone could make First Lady, you could.'

CHAPTER SEVEN

THE very next week, the great diva Adriana Crespi arrived to a fanfare of publicity. At a press conference she lost little time summoning Alix to her side.

'So you are the young lady who interviewed my Richard?'

Alix smiled and said yes, she was. Close too, the telltale age lines showed around the diva's eyes and mouth and throat, but she was still a magnificent-looking woman, with great flashing eyes, a big passionate mouth and a tall, voluptuous figure. She was superbly dressed and bejewelled as well, and the total effect was like seeing someone on the big screen after years of being glued to the television.

'It was really quite good,' Adriana said magnanimously. For a coloratura with a fantastic range she made full use of her rich, deep notes in her speaking voice. 'So how *is* he?'

For the life of her Alix couldn't control a stupid blush. 'Very well, signora.'

'Why did you automatically blame me for everything?' the great eyes flashed.

'Of course I didn't!' Alix answered, equally straightforwardly. 'You *had* to be mentioned, one of the greatest operatic sopranos in the world. . . .'

'The greatest!' Adriana interrupted a trifle balefully. As she spoke she drew a deep breath and her magnificent bosom swelled the line of her bronze silk blouse and lifted the long double string of pearls. 'Why isn't he here?'

'This is just for the media.'

'I want to see him.' The diva was still breathing deeply, much to the interest of scores of newsmen. 'Our tragedy was Richard's fault, without a doubt.'

'I'm sorry, signora,' Alix said with genuine sympathy. 'Both of you are such wonderful artists. It's a great honour to have you here.'

'How nice! *You* are nice,' Adriana said wonderingly. 'My enemies have told me you are one of Richard's women.' The beautifully cut nostrils flared.

'You can see for yourself that can't possibly be true!' Alix lifted sweetly innocent grey eyes, counting her lucky stars they *were* innocent. Adriana in a fury, bosom swelling and nostrils flaring, would rob anyone of courage. 'Actually, signora, if I could tell you this in confidence, I'm about to announce my engagement.'

She laughed a little shyly and Adriana leaned over and grasped her hand. A little too tightly for comfort. 'Be *happy*! I could see at a glance you are a really good girl, and good girls don't play around with other women's husbands.'

Apparently Adriana didn't remember that she and Richard were divorced. 'I want to see him,' she said. 'I'm sure you can get him a message.'

'He's been extremely unhappy, signora,' Alix said, suddenly protective of Richard. Not for anything would she have him driven back into his shell.

'And I haven't?' Adriana demanded with a great

deal of drama. 'I have *suffered*. Women always do. It is our greatest problem, how to bear the infidelity of men.'

'He told me he'd never been unfaithful to you,' Alix said gently, assuming this would quiet the diva down.

'*Lies!*' Adriana roared, then waved her fingers apologetically at all the turned heads. 'He was always very, very naughty.'

'I expect a lot of men are,' said Alix, thinking it would be terrible for such a woman to be betrayed. 'The thing is, *you* are the one who has the tremendous hold on him. He speaks of you constantly.' Even when he doesn't intend to, she thought. Personally Alix thought it was a terrible love-hate they would never work out.

'I am a beautiful woman,' Adriana said. 'I'm sure no one could say otherwise.'

'No one here,' Alix confirmed, catching Gary's sparkling blue eyes.

'I fell in love with Richard the very minute I saw him. I *adore* him!'

'It seems to me the very least you could do, signora, is tell him.'

'He has heard it time and time again!' The huge black eyes were mournful. 'I have had to sublimate my grief, pour my heart out in song, but Richard has withdrawn like the coward he is!'

Cowardice was catching, Alix thought. She was still seeing Adriana in a temper. Most men detested tantrums, and Adriana's would be full-blown affairs.

'You are a kind girl,' Adriana said, and once again

took Alix's hand. 'Young, lovely, about to be married. Take a message to Richard for me, from my heart. I *must* see him. We must forget the past.'

The past could very easily happen again, Alix thought wretchedly. Adriana's only hope was that Richard too was getting older. Eventually he would look nowhere else but to his wife.

'You will do this for me?' Alix had been silent so long, the diva stared anxiously into her face.

'I will carry your message, signora,' Alix said bravely. 'My only worry is that Mr Kaufmann (a diplomacy) has only just recently begun to come out of his shell. It would be a tragedy if he were driven back. For himself and for the world. He hasn't given a single performance in a long time.'

'You mean you haven't heard him play?' Adriana blinked her thick, sweeping lashes.

'I mean his public haven't heard him play,' Alix said winningly, careful to keep her expression that of an about-to-be-engaged girl.

'I will not take responsibility. *No!*' Adriana's full mouth turned down. 'Always he blames me. I took care of him like a mother. But what happens? As youth fades, men look elsewhere.'

'I don't know, signora,' Alix shook her head regretfully. 'All I do know is, you were, are still, the most important figure in his life. A magnificent obsession!'

'A very nice child!' Adriana smiled on her blazingly. 'I feel I can trust you. I've said things to you I have said to no one else. Some people move us. Most don't. I have punished Richard enough; he has punished me. It is time for us now to come together again, make music—*love*!'

'Could we have some more pictures here, Signora Crespi?' the bravest of the pressmen called.

'Always they call me,' said Adriana, 'but I am part of all the world.' She stood up and straightened the skirt of her brilliantly designed three-piece suit. She had fabulous long legs, in excellent shape. 'You may reach me at my hotel.'

When Alix told Carl, he laughed. 'God, they're bent on devouring one another!'

'So what about Richard?' She came round his desk to stare out the huge plate glass window.

'He has nothing to lose,' Carl answered cynically. 'He was better with her than without her.'

'I feel sort of responsible.'

'Oh, sure,' he said dryly. 'Don't think you're going to prop Richard up. Leave it to a strong woman like La Crespi.'

'She's a splendid-looking creature,' Alix said broodingly. 'Funny and fierce.'

'One wouldn't expect her to be ordinary!' Carl drew a number of heavy red lines through some copy he was reading. 'Why don't you let them work it out for themselves? I'm glad to say he's already decided for himself it would be useless to look at you.'

'I don't know how his other ladies had the nerve to cross Adriana Crespi,' Alix gave a shaky little laugh. 'I was even chicken enough to tell her I was about to become engaged.'

'*Chicken!*' He reached out his arms and pulled her forcibly on to his knee. 'You mean you were thinking of your health?'

'Yes, sir,' she said fervently. 'I wouldn't like to be the other woman with Adriana around.'

'Talk about insults!' He made no move to release her.

Alix turned her face to stare into his black eyes. 'She called him her husband as though they'd never been divorced.'

'Italians tend to think like that.' The hand around her waist moved higher. 'Often makes me wonder if I have Italian blood myself.'

'Of course.' She was surprised into really staring at him; taking his features apart. He was very dark, black hair, large eyes as black as coal, hewn features rather than chiselled, an excellent mouth and teeth. It was a face to look at, flaunting its masculinity. A Mediterranean face really. She had never quite got used to it. Foreign. In the stillness, with his brilliant black eyes on her, she traced the shape of his mouth. After a minute she began to feel that liquid fire and she wanted to kiss him.

'Go on,' he said with a remote kind of mockery.

'What?' She took her eyes from his mouth to look into his fathomless eyes.

'Kiss me. You want to.'

'You're very conceited.' Her soft voice was husky.

'Never with you, Conroy,' he said dryly. 'I'm afraid of you.'

'Me?' She laughed as though it were a joke. 'I'm a push-over, God knows.'

'For *me*?' He got his hard hand beneath her chin. 'Are you already resenting your promise?'

Why did she always tremble when he touched her? It was sheer black magic. 'Of course,' she answered gently. 'Why do you ever bother to ask me?'

His smile did fantastic things to his hard, sombre face. 'Little cat.'

'Don't you know *anything* about your parents?' Once started on her close examination of his features, she continued. He had very fine-grained, dark olive skin, the kind of beard that came up very easily. He would look rather splendid with a beard, gloriously male, only she didn't fancy close contact with a bearded husband.

There, she had thought of it herself. *Husband*.

'What are you thinking about?' Carl asked curiously.

'I don't want you to grow a beard. Even though it would suit you.'

'All right.' He brushed a hand over her hair. 'I know you like me just the way I am.'

'Did no one tell you anything, Carl? The nuns?'

'About what?' he asked lightly, though his black eyes were shadowed.

'Don't you want to talk about it?' Unbelievably she was as comfortable on his knee as she had ever been in her life.

'There's nothing to talk about, darling. My mother was a woman, I suppose, my father some hot-blooded male. Neither wanted to keep me. I was rather like Moses, set afloat.'

'Are you Catholic? You talk about the nuns.'

'No. There must be something lacking in me, Alix. I don't believe in anything.'

'That's not right!' Her silver eyes kindled. 'You believe in family. You want one, right?'

'In return for which, I'll slave for you!' He smiled at

her, but there was a ruthless determination in his face.

'What you want,' she said with a mixture of despair, comfort and humour,' is the love of a good woman. All the natural softness has been drummed out of you.'

'Then you can't know how I feel inside!' For a moment his eyes held hers and she felt if she looked deep enough she might be able to discover at least a few of his closest held secrets. The obvious results of his deprived childhood, the self-reliance, the hardness and ruthless determination were only a part of the real man. Carl loved beauty and spent considerable sums of money to possess it; he made love with a sweetness and an artistry that would surely make a slave of her; and now that she really thought about it, he went right out of his way to create opportunities for talent. Peter had told her he still visited his old orphanage, and she was certain he never went empty-handed. He was really worth knowing. She *wanted* to know him.

Only when the phone rang did she come out of her reverie.

'Danning,' he said.

She went to move away, but he still held her. 'Didn't I tell you to ring me this morning?' he said shortly. 'I want all the technical details cleared up. What spies? In my office? *Hell*!'

Alix tried to move again and this time he let her. In any case, she had work to do herself.

All in all, Peter spent three weeks at the Gold Coast and when he came home he was so tall and brown and golden, Alix felt her eyes fill with tears.

'I swear you've grown!' she said, when they had hugged one another.

'You're the shrimp in this family.' He loped along beside her as they walked to the car park. 'I had a wonderful time, but I'm glad to be home. I missed you.'

'Tell me everything!' She smiled at him, feeling so happy there were bubbles in her blood. How handsome he was getting, how like their dear father.

He talked all the way home, and it was only over dinner that Alix was able to tell him her news.

'What would you say if I suddenly became engaged?'

'I don't believe it!'

Certainly not wonderful! from the look on his face.

'You're totally surprised, aren't you?' she said worriedly, watching him try to hide his upset. Just to prove it he had stopped eating his chocolate nut sundae.

'It surely couldn't be that Kaufmann character?' He got up and moved aimlessly to the kitchen dresser.

'*No!*' Her voice sounded shocked.

'Not Guy!' The contempt in his voice left her in little doubt of his opinion of her ex-fiancé.

'Really I should have told you at once,' she said. 'It's Carl.'

'*Carl?*' He made an incoherent sound that could have been joy or shock. 'Can we start again? *You're* getting engaged to *Carl?*'

'Yes.' She looked up at him anxiously, her heart in her eyes.

'How has this happened?' He picked up his ice-cream and began eating it again. 'I thought you and

Carl were in some kind of contest of wills or something.'

'He won.'

'Congratulations!' At the sudden blaze of pleasure on his face, her head fell into her hands.

'Oh, darling!' she sighed.

'You're happy, aren't you, Sissy?'

He hadn't called her Sissy for years. Even his voice sounded years younger.

'Of course I am,' she lifted her head to smile into his baffled face. 'I was just worried how *you* would take the news.'

'But I like Carl! He's a great guy—worth at least a hundred of Guy any day. I thought for one terrible minute you were going to tell me it was on again between you two. He wouldn't have any place for *me*. I'd be shunted off to boarding school at the drop of a hat.'

'Not while I was around.'

'Anyway,' Peter said, 'we don't have to worry. You never were convincing telling me how you didn't like Carl. Of all the men in the world I think he suits you the best. He's strong, a rock. You won't have to struggle any more.'

The following day, with Peter told, Alix and Carl announced their engagement. As she suspected, there was no choosing the ring. He slipped the most exquisitely romantic ruby and diamond ring over her finger and that was that. Engaged. Even Val managed to offer her best wishes, stopping by Alix's desk.

'It really is *gorgeous*!' she said, tawny eyes narrowing assessingly over the ring. 'You're a real cool one, aren't you? None of us ever suspected.'

'I did.' Gary spun around in his chair. 'Wait until I tell Marj, she'll be thrilled!'

'So when's the wedding?' Val sat down uninvited.

'We haven't decided.' Alix didn't want to be pressured into any wedding. An engagement was enough.

'I never did thank you for not dobbing me in to Carl,' Val said wryly. 'Me and my ambitions! Sometimes they get me into trouble. Anyway,' she added brightly, 'you'll very likely be giving up your job?'

It was a cry for assurance, but Alix couldn't give it. Carl was so new to her. So strange, yet familiar. 'We haven't made any plans yet,' she said lightly, and turned to Gary. 'Now what night is it you want me to baby-sit the kids?'

'You don't have to. Not now, an engaged woman!' Gary grinned.

'Wednesday, wasn't it?'

'Yes, ma'am,' Gary said.

Because Alix hadn't told Richard in advance, had in fact been dreading it, for some unknown reason he seemed very much hurt.

'I thought we were friends,' he said, looking suddenly tired and old. '*Good* friends.'

'Of course we are, Richard.' They had come together for lunch.

'Then couldn't I have been the first to know?'

'Peter is the *first* person in my life,' she said gently.

'What an odd answer!' He looked across at her with hooded eyes. 'Not that Carl isn't a fine chap.' It sounded somewhat petulant.

'I want you to be happy for me,' she said truthfully.

'Oh, I am!' He frowned and took her hand, staring down at the beautiful ring. 'That's an extremely fine stone. Where did you get it?'

'I didn't ask.'

'Odd,' he said again. 'Ah well, let me raise my glass in a toast. To the happy couple!'

'What's the matter?' she enquired, sensing his wretched state of mind.

'If I'd only been a few years younger, I'd have asked for your hand first.'

'Oh, Richard!' What else could she say? He wasn't shattered at all, only vaguely resentful. 'Won't you *please* give Adriana an answer? It's a terrible thing to make a woman like that beg!'

'No more terrible than what she did to me!' His eyes were bleak in his pale oval face. Except for his hands, which looked immensely strong, he was rather a frail person in the sense one thought he could easily succumb to a fatal disease.

'She told me, Richard, she adores you,' Alix said seriously, the role of mediator pressed on her.

'She has a funny way of showing it,' Richard murmured cynically. 'I tell you, I was tied to a mad woman!'

'Who could blame her for being jealous?'

Richard took this as a compliment, his mouth curving in a faintly complacent smile. 'Because of Adriana, I abandoned my career.'

'Was it Adriana,' she asked gravely, 'or was it fear?'

His dark eyes were more guarded than ever. 'What on earth do you mean?'

'Artists of your calibre are extremely sensitive

people, perfectionists. Might it be better to say sub-consciously you sought a period of renewal?'

'You don't know what you're talking about,' he shrugged it off with assumed casualness—a casualness that didn't show in his eyes or the strain of his expression. 'The answer is quite simple. Adriana was bad for me.'

'She told me she's suffered as well.'

'May she choke,' Richard said pleasantly. 'Preferably when she's about to hit top E.'

'So the answer is no.'

'No matter how you argue.' Richard beckoned to the waiter for coffee. 'It seems to me, Alix, you have some fondness for my ex-wife?'

'I've only met her a few times and spoken to her on the phone, but yes, I *do* like her. She's a spellbinding woman. Not just in her singing, but in her presence.'

'And you believe she's serious when she says she still loves me?'

'So far as I can tell. I'm not an expert, Richard, on human emotions.'

'Yet you're in love yourself?' He shot her a piercing glance.

What was she? Alix thought, beginning to become distressed. She had no idea of her real feelings for Carl. He wasn't in any way the sort of man she had thought of as her type. Loving her father so much, as a little girl growing up, she had seen her ideal man as being tall and lean and fair with an inbuilt elegance. Guy had been sufficiently smooth and good-looking to compel her attention, only Guy had been worthless, a man of no substance.

In truth her heart was in confusion.

'Well, aren't you?' Richard persisted, secretly piqued that there was another man in her life she found more attractive. A long-time fascinator of women, he found it was hard to lose one's grip. Alix was looking very lovely today, perhaps a trifle too young, but very blonde and patrician in a cream silk dress that he liked. 'Answer me, Alix, you must think of me truly as your friend.'

To the couple coming into the main dining room of that very exclusive restaurant, it looked like an intense tête-à-tête. Alix's golden head was bent, and her expression was sad and introspective. Richard Kaufmann, the most talked-of man in town, was holding her hand, his silver-winged head bent protectively towards hers.

'*Gran Dio!*' exclaimed Adriana, feeling such a constriction around the heart she thought it not unlikely at her age that she could have a heart attack.

'Steady!' The tall powerfully built man just slightly behind her caught her arm.

'And I *trusted* her!'

'You have every reason to,' the man replied rather curtly. 'I suggest you act the great lady. Every eye in this dining room is now on you.'

Only Richard and Alix hadn't seen them, and after a minute, Alix did.

'Good God!' she exclaimed, drawing a long jagged breath. Above and beyond Adriana, she had noticed Carl's eyes.

'What is it?' Instinctively Richard turned his head.

The waiter, bringing the coffee, backed away. Adriana had received a lot of press and T.V. coverage since she had arrived, and the waiter, being Italian, had very quick perceptions. Here was the ex-wife, the husband, a beautiful blonde girl-friend. . . .

Adriana swept to their table with Carl in attendance. She was wearing a great picture hat festooned with magnolias, a diamond-clasped angel skin necklace, angel skin eardrops with diamond clasps, a wonderfully simple Dior dress, and she looked a marvel.

'*Caro!*' Her thrilling voice rang out.

To Richard's credit, he was equal to the occasion—no doubt from long practice. He rose to his feet, kissed Adriana's hand and as she drew him relentlessly towards her they eventually kissed one another on both cheeks.

Now that the moment of crisis had passed, waiters scurried. Two extra chairs were easily accommodated to the table.

'This fiancé of yours,' Adriana said intensely to Alix, 'I particularly like. He's a fighter. He wouldn't sulk and have a nervous breakdown and run away to another country.'

'Dear Father in Heaven!' muttered Richard.

Alix sat on the edge of her chair, rigid with embarrassment, but still her downcast face looked beautiful.

'I think, if you don't mind,' said Carl, 'I'll take my fiancée off. That is, signora, if you're beyond help.'

Adriana turned to him with a curiously apologetic look. 'I promise. I *promise*. I shall behave.'

'I think you'd better take her all the same,' Richard said maliciously.

'It seems to me,' Carl said forcefully, 'there's something the matter with both of you. Why do you pretend?'

'*Please*, Richard!' Adriana's lustrous dark eyes grew even more lustrous with tears. 'I only want to talk to you.'

'But, darling, you're breaking up a party.'

'No, she's not!' Carl deliberately took Alix's hand. 'Let's make one thing perfectly clear. Alix is not part of this and I won't have her subjected to the least public scandal. I suggest you both try to act like two disciplined adults—at least in the name of the love you once had for each other.'

Adriana blushed, which made her look younger and softer, and Richard looked vaguely shamefaced. 'If you believe it possible, Carl, then it is.'

For thirty minutes more Alix and Carl witnessed the breakdown in both Adriana's and Richard's defences. Having expended most of their hate, it seemed, they were free to love again.

When finally Carl deemed it safe to leave, reminiscences had set in, indissoluble links.

'Why don't you go home?' Carl said moodily, when they were out on the street. 'You seem played out.'

'Are we going to take up where Richard and Adriana left off?'

'Not *me*, madonna. I've had enough unhappiness to last me a lifetime.'

He put her in a cab, gave the driver instructions and a five-dollar note and walked away.

Alix was played out; she realised it now. It had been very wearing trying to effect a reconciliation between two high-voltage people. Not that she had any great hopes for that same reconciliation, human nature being what it is. She would have to do what Carl suggested, leave them work it out for themselves. The only really exciting thing was that, not to be outdone, Adriana had consented to give an exclusive interview to *Impact*, with the natural assumption, of course, that she would feature on the cover. She had even brought with her from America a wonderful new gown for that very purpose; something dateless, for the cover was bound to become a collector's edition.

It was to be one of those days, for by five o'clock in the evening Peter still hadn't returned home. Not that five o'clock was so late, but Alix had allowed him to go to a movie with Rusty and the morning session would have come out around about two o'clock. Her very last words to him had been to come right on home, and Peter never, *never* disobeyed her.

By half past five, she was so agitated she rang Helen. Peter was all she had in the world and she couldn't help the way she had become over-protective, over-anxious.

Helen was hiding her own anxieties with some effort. 'I expect they've met up with their friends. Time flies, they could be just looking around the shops.'

'But they've closed, Helen.'

'Only just.' Helen spoke soothingly, realising only too well Alix's fears. 'I'm sure they'll be home any minute. It will be light for another hour.'

They spoke for a minute more, then Alix went to stand out on the balcony. Peter was getting such a big boy she couldn't treat him like a baby. Helen was right; it was still broad daylight and he had probably forgotten the time.

Not Peter! an inner voice said, crushing her. The events of their life had made Peter very responsible. He knew she would worry, which was one reason he stuck exactly to time. Even when he was out on his bike he was never away for long.

Her beautiful ring caught the light, and she stared down at with a frowning expression. She was engaged, which meant she could and should call on her fiancé for support. The terrible thing was, she didn't really think of Carl as her fiancé at all. The whole situation was wrong. She should never have allowed herself to become engaged to him. The basic fact was that he wanted her and he was so strong and determined she had resigned herself to her fate, like some pitiable girl in a primitive culture. She had a problem, and she stared bewildered at the empty street.

Where was Peter?

When the phone rang, she nearly jumped out of her skin. 'Hello?' Her voice was wobbly with nerves.

'Alix?'

She forced herself to speak calmly, responding to the hard note of enquiry. 'Oh, Carl!'

'What's the matter, what is it?'

'Peter hasn't arrived home.' She sank down on to the phone chair, thinking for the millionth time how hard it was.

'So it's not six o'clock.' His voice sounded very calm.

'He went to a morning movie with Rusty. The

session would have been out around two and I told him to come straight home. Peter always does what I tell him. *Always.*'

He didn't answer for a minute, perhaps thinking. 'What movie?'

She told him, feeling the nerves in her stomach jumping. This was what tragedy had done to her. She was going to pieces.

'Have you rung Rusty's place?' Carl was asking.

'I'd better get off the phone,' she said, 'in case Helen wants to ring me.'

'Don't panic, Alix,' he said firmly. 'Peter is a very sensible boy. Any number of minor things could have happened. He's run into friends . . . missed a bus. You can't allow yourself to jump to the worst possible conclusions. Go and make yourself a cup of tea and I'll be right over.'

When she put down the receiver, she sat for a few moments with her head bowed. Keep calm, she thought. Peter is a sensible boy.

She could hardly remember making the tea, or drinking it, but when she heard the Jaguar pull up and she knew the special sound of it, she flew on to the balcony.

Carl opened up one door and got out. Peter opened up the other.

'Thank God!' She felt tremulous with relief. She didn't wait until they caught the lift, she went down to meet them.

'*Peter!*' She didn't even glance at Carl. Peter's face was very white and what few freckles he had were standing out across his nose. 'What's happened? I've been so worried!'

'Easy!' Carl took hold of both their arms and put them in the lift. 'Peter's perfectly all right.'

'Yes, I am!' Peter looked across at his sister, his blue eyes willing her to calm down. 'Some lunatic. . . .'

'We'll wait until we get upstairs, shall we?' Carl pressed the boy's arm.

'*Tell* me!' Alix was looking bewildered and frightened.

The lift stopped and Carl touched Peter's shoulder. 'Go in and sit down.'

In the passageway he took Alix's hand firmly. 'The boys had a slight accident about an hour before they were due to come home. A car collected a few people on a pedestrian crossing. Miraculously no one was seriously hurt, the car wasn't going fast enough, but the boys and a couple of other people were jolted and shocked. A cruising police car took them to the hospital to make sure nothing was wrong.'

'And how did you find out?' She stopped walking and stared at him.

'I made a few very quick phone calls. Incidentally, a policeman friend of mine has run Rusty home.'

'He's all right?' Her grey eyes were huge.

'Just shaken, like Peter. They took a tumble and they got a fright.'

'Oh, dear!'

In the living room, Peter was sprawled in the most comfortable chair with his feet up. 'I guess I was born lucky!' Now that the worst of the shock had passed, he was ready to give a detailed account.

Alix didn't answer; she couldn't. She slumped into the chair facing him. 'I *knew* there was something wrong.'

'I dragged Rusty away so fast only the bumper bar hit us. He said his brakes failed, but I'll bet they didn't.'

'They didn't,' Carl told him soberly.

'There's a lot of excitement goes on in hospitals,' Peter said. 'Even while I was there. . . .'

'I'd better go and ring Helen,' Alix said quickly. She knew the sort of thing that went on in hospitals. Saving lives, the terrible moments when death defeated human hands.

'*I'll* ring Rusty's mother,' said Carl, and got a hand on her shoulder. 'Just sit quietly with Peter. Or if you can't do that, get us both dinner. I'm hungry and I bet Peter is too.'

'It takes you like that,' Peter called after them confirmingly. 'I haven't had anything except a malted milk since I left home.'

'What's the number?' Carl looked back at the boy, as Alix was looking around her rather dazedly.

'But you rang from the hospital.'

'I'll ring again.'

Alix was assembling the salad ingredients when he came back into the kitchen. 'Well?' She lifted her eyes to stare at his tall, powerful figure.

'Rusty is home, ready like Peter to make a story of it.'

'They could have been killed!' Suddenly she was crying, weeping like her heart was about to break.

'*Alix!*' In a second Carl had her cradled against him, and Peter appeared wide-eyed at the door.

'I *told* you she'd get a fright!'

'All right, so you make the salad.'

'Don't think I can't,' Peter grinned, and as he went

past them patted Alix's shoulder. 'I'm really all right, Sis.' He cleared his throat. '*Really.*'

'Good boy!' Carl smiled down at the handsome young face. 'What are we having with this salad?'

There was no doubt Alix wasn't about to cook with them. She was crying her heart out.

'Steak.' Peter threw open the refrigerator. 'Say, this is exciting! All the top chefs in the world are men.'

Even Alix was becoming alarmed at her own breakdown and she choked her sobs into hiccoughing gasps. She could conclude from the way Carl was comforting her that he had had a lot of experience with the orphanage babies. For a big man he had a magically gentle hand and the most soothing action. . . .

They were seated in the big rocker armchair in the living room, she cradled on his knees and he apparently not in the least perturbed by a woman's tempestuous tears.

'Cry it out,' he said into the silky top of her head.

'I'm sorry!' she exclaimed, over and over. Once started, it was hard to pull out of a crying spree.

Peter looked in on them once or twice, decked out in an apron that said BONZER COOK, then he was called away to check on the progress of the steak and the tiny new potatoes.

'I'm ashamed of myself,' Alix muttered, when she could finally lift her face.

He looked down at her in silence, not prompting her immediate responses.

'It's just that Peter is so precious to me,' she said emotionally. 'He's all I've got.'

'Except for me,' said Carl in an expressionless voice, without reproach.

'Oh, Carl!' A sudden horror struck at her. Could she be hurting him? She *couldn't*. He didn't love her.

'You're quite a girl, Conroy,' he said dryly, gazing at her closely with his black eyes. 'You've been crying for a good ten minutes and you haven't even got red eyes. That's really something.'

She was still staring at him uncertainly. 'I know you're my fiancé.'

'You do?' He got his hand under her chin and tilted her face.

'I need *time*, Carl.'

He stopped the downward direction of a tear with his finger and instead of wiping it away, he put it in his mouth. 'Alix's tears. Would you ever cry for me?'

His black eyes were the most vital, living eyes she had ever seen. Adriana's eyes were dark and very beautiful; Richard's too were dark brown, but she had never seen eyes like Carl's. But there was the paradox. Brilliant as they were, she couldn't read the expressions they held in their depths.

'We're a strange pair, aren't we?' she said softly. 'I think you only want me because I've got long blonde hair. Probably I look a little like someone in a story book you read as a child.'

'Except we didn't have story books,' he smiled at her slightly. 'I made you up.'

Melancholy would suit his dark, brooding looks very well, except he wasn't the type to give in to it. If she lifted her face a fraction, she could touch his mouth with her own. He wanted his way and nothing else. He wanted her. *Why?*

When Peter came back into the room to announce that he was about to serve dinner, he found them staring into one another's faces in silence.

'Gee, isn't someone going to turn on the light and set the table?' he prompted. 'I've got everything just right. All except the plates.'

When he turned and flicked the light switch, Alix looked dazzled. 'I'm sorry,' she said, and scrambled off Carl's knee. 'I'll attend to it.'

'Will it be all right,' unexpectedly Peter put the question to Carl, 'if I have a glass of wine tonight?'

'A small glass won't hurt.' Carl put his arm around the boy's thin shoulders and led him back into the kitchen. 'Tell me where it is, and I'll open it.'

As a first effort, Peter's offering was highly satisfactory. He had forgotten to put salt in with the potatoes, the salad dressing was a little unusual, but the steaks were cooked to perfection. All through the meal he smiled at both of them and accepted their compliments, deviating awhile to relate some of the best parts of the movie he and Rusty had seen. The whiteness and the shock had vanished from his face, but Alix insisted he sit and talk to Carl while she cleared away the dishes. If nothing else, she knew her brother and her fiancé were highly compatible. Wasn't that a good reason why she had allowed herself to become engaged to Carl in the first place?

She sighed over the bubbling suds, thousands of questions going round in her head, and as she did so Carl spoke behind her.

'So what are you thinking about now?' He opened a drawer and pulled out a clean tea towel.

'That's all right,' she said abruptly.

'I'll do it. Peter has gone off to have his shower. It might be best if he has an early night.'

'Yes, Big Brother.'

'Would you rather I were that instead of what I am?'

'To tell the truth,' she said a little shakily, 'I'm rather confused.'

'You think I've forced you into this?' He lifted a dinner plate out of the rack, dried it and put it away efficiently. From what she had seen of his apartment he was fanatically neat. Neater than she was.

She didn't answer but bit her lip.

'This could do with another scrub,' he said, and slipped a bread and butter plate back into the washing water.

'Oh, shut up!' Alix clicked her tongue irritably. There was only the tiniest little smudge of grease.

'I run a tight ship,' he said, and laughed.

'I expect you'd drive me crazy!' she said feelingly.

'I intend to. Excuse me, please.' He moved her aside firmly. 'I'll wash, you wipe!'

'Oh, damn, you can do the lot!' Alix pulled off her gloves and threw them down, grey eyes flashing silver, soft mouth mutinous.

'Oh no, you don't!' He caught her and pulled her hard into his arms. 'You're not abandoning the field.'

'I *hate* you, Carl!' she said stormily.

'Thanks, but I'm going to console myself.'

'Oh, God!' It was all she had time to murmur before he kissed her mouth.

She stood rigid for a moment, locked in his arms then like always, her real self slipped away and she was left with that other one. The one who responded to Carl; who opened her mouth to his consuming passion, knees buckling. If an atomic bomb had gone off, it wouldn't have distracted her.

He moved them both around so he was leaning against the dresser, never taking his mouth from her own. It even seemed her desire ran parallel with his and kissing was rapidly becoming not enough.

'*Alix!*' He turned his mouth away from hers for a moment and his voice sound anguished.

'What do you *do* to me?' Her skin was burning.

'I don't know if I can take too much of this!' His strong arm around her waist was preventing her from falling.

Alix didn't know if she could either, but she was strangely reluctant to tell him.

'How long?' he muttered in that same harsh tone.

'What can I tell you?' She bent her head and let it fall against his chest. 'It doesn't make any sense the way I feel about you.'

'You want me,' he said boldly. 'You want me very much, but there's two people inside you, Alix, and one I can't control.'

'So what do you do?' She lifted her head, willing the dizziness to go away. Carl always made her so dizzy. It was like losing contact with reality.

'You know what they say,' he said, not without humour. 'Plenty of cold showers, plenty of runs around the park. I've never wanted a woman in my life the way I want you.'

'Then I'm surprised I lasted a week,' she answered tartly.

'Maybe I *love* you,' he said jeeringly. 'Respect you. Don't want to hurt you.'

She swallowed at the note in his voice when he said *love*. If a man like Carl Danning loved you, you would be loved for life. Failing that, there was what they had now.

'Well?' he muttered, his hands hard at her waist.

'Maybe for both our sakes,' she said seriously, 'I should let you sleep with me. Then your fever will burn out.'

'So I dare you to!' His eyes were so fathomless it was too easy to drown in them. Just the way he looked at her fanned every last flame of latent sensuality. She trembled violently and he pulled her right up against him, moulding her slender woman's body to his own.

She was sinking into layers of cloud, closing her eyes. '*Don't*, Carl!'

'What do you think of yourself now?' He wouldn't let her get away.

Surrender, she thought convulsively. This was so much heaven, it was hell!

'One night soon, I'm going to take you,' he said sombrely against her throat. 'I'll even tell you the night. The night that we're married. I never figured I was so proper. I never have been, but you're going to come to me the way I want and I'm going to be the first and last man in your life.'

'*Alix!*'

Peter's voice brought them abruptly apart.

'In the kitchen,' she called, a little hoarsely.

'Oh, you're still here!' Peter came in to join them looking pleased.

'Your hair's wet,' Alix said anxiously.

'Don't fuss. It'll dry.' Peter looked from one to the other, then at the twin sinks. 'Gosh, haven't you finished the washing up yet?'

'We're a newly engaged couple,' Carl's taut face relaxed, 'haven't you heard?'

'Not kissing, you mean?' Peter blinked.

'What else?' Carl leaned over and ruffled the boy's blond damp head. 'It's all very boring at your age, but it sort of comes to all of us.'

Peter went a boyish pink and laughed. 'We'll, I'm glad it came to you two.'

'Thanks.' Carl smiled at him with an odd softening in his brilliant eyes.

Yes, he really likes children, Alix thought, and turned away. Which was all very well, except surely he didn't expect her to found a dynasty? Whatever her feelings for him, they were unparalleled in her existence.

CHAPTER EIGHT

THE gala opening of Adriana's single performance as Violetta in *Traviata* was one of the greatest festive occasions the city had seen for some time. It only needed the presence of the Queen and the dashing Duke of Edinburgh to have made it truly splendid, but unfortunately the Royal couple were not due in the city for another month. Nevertheless all the T.V. cameras were out, there were sightseers galore and the long line of celebrities who walked smilingly up to the concert hall were all very stylishly turned out. Many of them were even opera fans. Everyone knew Adriana was a possessor of a voice of great beauty and power, but she was also that rare thing, a person of great glamour. Legendary her passionately appealing Violetta might be, what was more exciting was the real-life rumours that flew about her. After all, there was no substitute for reality. Adriana hadn't been interviewed by *Impact* as yet, but everyone knew, from her appearance on the top rating national T.V. current affairs programme, she was a lady of wit and style and grand passions—to a lot of people's minds, one of the prerequisites of a great diva.

It wasn't until Richard arrived with the very pretty girl he had met at the Pearsons' party that Alix knew the first pang of anxiety.

'Good grief!' She clutched at Carl's arm, forcing him to look in the direction of her gaze.

Even Carl drew a ragged breath. Trouper that she was, Adriana had been known to address the audience from on stage. 'There's something about Richard that bothers me. Why the hell did he have to bring that girl here?'

'If anyone it should have been a distinguished old lady.' Adriana had told her Richard's love for her was alive again and flourishing. Now *this!*

'Good evening! Alix . . . Carl. . . .' Richard and his companion made their way to the adjoining seats. 'You know Jenny, don't you?'

Jenny gave them a brilliant smile and a breathless, 'Hullo!'

This was utterly wrong. Alix couldn't keep the dismay out of her eyes. 'Have you seen Adriana?' she asked.

'I sent her magnificent white roses, failing camellias,' Richard said blandly. 'Really, it's such a crush!' He lifted his handsome head and gazed all about him. 'I believe she's far from happy with one of her costumes—had the dresser in tears. Of course the real problem is her fluctuating weight.'

'Isn't it exciting!' Jenny interrupted, not having heard a single word.

'Very!' Carl smiled at her with a peculiarly ironic light in his eye. 'You look very pretty.'

'Thank you.' Jenny gave him another brilliant smile. It made no sense at all why the great Richard Kaufmann had asked her to accompany him, but she was going to make the most of it. 'You look divine yourself!'

'How *could* you, Richard?' Alix whispered in a

shocked aside. 'You know Adriana. You know how she feels and reacts. Besides, this is her great night.'

'Cheer up, pet,' Richard said lightly. 'Adriana is quite used to enduring my callousness. How do you know, for that matter, if I'm not testing?'

'Testing?' Alix stared into his face, trying to exact the truth.

'I have some vague idea of making Adriana prove herself.' Richard rolled up his programme and hit his knee with it. 'I can't live the rest of my life under the crushing weight of her jealousies. She's either going to act like a sensible woman, or attempt to bring me down in flames.'

'Couldn't you have chosen another night to provoke her?'

'I had a great craving to do it tonight,' Richard told her bluntly. 'I assume we're all going along to Lady Halford's supper party?'

'If we get that far!' Carl said dryly. 'I can't help feeling sorry for your sweet little guinea-pig.'

'Heavens, yes!' Alix stared across at Jenny's pretty, blazing face, but Jenny was engrossed in the glamour of the occasion, trying to identify the woman, definitely not his wife, who was with the millionaire entrepreneur Roger Matthews.

The Governor arrived, his lady, both looking resplendent. Everyone applauded fervently. After all, it was an occasion. Ten minutes later, the curtain went up.

Without even knowing she was doing it, Alix slipped her hand into Carl's. Whatever happened, he was as calm and dependable as a rock. To her mind, what Richard sought to do was dangerous, a mad gamble. It might seem right and natural to him, but Adriana would take it as another instance of betrayal. She could even shriek it from the stage.

She shuddered and Carl tightened his grip on her hand. She was wearing a very beautiful white dress, her mother's pearls, and because the occasion was formal she had her hair styled in the latest version of a chignon, adorned with tiny white flowers and two silky curling tendrils pulled out to frame her face. Peter, with brotherly enthusiasm, had told her she looked super-cool, Carl, the instant she had come to the door, told her she looked exquisite, but now she felt as shaken and frail as the second act Violetta. Richard's action had genuinely shocked her. Had he no fear of what Adriana might do?'

'*Relax!*' Carl saw the anguish on her pure profile. 'Adriana is an artist above all else!'

When Adriana came on to the stage in her magnificent gown, the audience crashed into a thrilling round of applause; not as much perhaps as they reserved for their own La Stupenda, but enough to make the ears ring.

'My God, isn't she glorious!' Richard whispered fervently, his dark face alight.

'Glorious!' Quite suddenly Alix wasn't so worried. At that moment Richard had eyes for no one but the beautiful woman up there on the stage. More, emotion caught hold of him and he stood up and applauded.

Emotion, or calculation, Alix couldn't decide. Adriana had spotted him, her great eyes brilliant and enormous with the heavy theatrical make-up. She blew a kiss with her hand, then her eyes moved along the line, by passing Carl and Alix and settling on Jenny's young, peachy face.

Richard sat down and took Jenny's hand.

Oh, what have you done? Alix thought, feeling a tightness in her chest. It was wicked of Richard a cruel, savage test. It would take a psychiatrist to work both of them out. Adriana was a great artist, a woman, and not so young.

She was an artist first!

Adriana turned, lifted pearly white arms and launched into song, the beauty of her voice so powerful, so round and gorgeous, she lifted the audience out of their seats.

'Well done!' said Richard in an intensely emotive hiss, 'but the true test is yet to come.'

All in all, if not perhaps vocally, it turned out to be the most moving performance of Adriana's operatic life. The audience wept with her, some, like Jenny, quite openly. It wasn't Adriana Crespi up there, but the beautiful, long-suffering, dying Violetta Valéry. On stage, made up, she dropped a good twenty years and everyone loved her—Alfredo, who was in fine voice, Richard, whose dark eyes glittered with a fierce pride.

'I've never seen anything so beautiful in my life!' Jenny said mistily.

On stage, Adriana with a magnificent sheaf of flowers in her arms, sank into a wonderful deep curtsy.

Further bursts of applause were released. The leading critic in the front stalls was moved to stand up and shout, 'Bravo!'

'Some lady!' Carl, also on his feet, turned to smile at Alix.

She didn't answer, the palms of her hands smarting, but her glowing face showed her own response. She had never seen such a wonderful singing actress in her life. She could only pray Adriana would be able to keep it up for the rest of the night.

The lavish after-performance supper party was held at the harbour-front mansion of Lady Halford, a sixtyish widow of great wealth and a frantically active social life, a genuine patron of the arts and a very nice woman as well. About fifty people had been invited back to meet the guest of honour and though Adriana didn't arrive for a good hour, no one stopped talking about her thrilling performance. Beatrice Halford, who had always wanted to sing and never could no matter how much she could afford it, induced Richard to go to the piano, so when Adriana finally arrived she did so to an impassioned medley of *Traviata*'s main arias.

'Either way,' said Carl in a voice of dark humour, 'this is going to be a night to remember!'

Alix had expected Adriana to sweep in on the crest of the wave of her great triumph, but Adriana looked tired and for a woman of statuesque proportions surprisingly vulnerable and appealing. She wore a very understated gown, a minimum of make-up and her wonderful mane of hair drawn back from her face to show the natural nobility of the bone structure.

'Thank you. Thank you.' She turned the palms of her hands up expressively as everyone cheered her arrival.

'She looks tragic,' Alix whispered to Carl, her soft heart turning over.

'Don't forget she's a good actress.'

Jenny, her pretty young face alight with admiration, was standing beside Richard at the piano. She knew nothing whatever of classical music, though she had grown closer to it tonight, and the last thing she would have liked to have seen was this great lady hurt.

'Someone should have warned Jenny,' said Alix, feeling anxious.

'You surely don't think Adriana is going to attack her?' Carl kept a social smile on his face while he moved them both a few feet closer the piano.

Richard had reached the last big, beautiful crashing chord and Beatrice Halford called out fondly, 'Magic fingers!'

'He's dangerous!' said Alix in a shaken whisper. 'I don't think he wants a peaceful solution to their problem at all.'

'Could be.' Carl shook his dark head, wondering at that moment, why anyone would want to make trouble for anyone else.

It was impossible to read anything behind Adriana's faintly weary expression. As Richard stood up, super-handsome and arty in his black dinner suit with an elaborately ruffled shirt, she moved towards him, caught his head between her two hands and gave him a long, deliberate kiss.

'*Contact!*' Carl said to Alix, and laughed gently beneath his breath.

In the beautiful bright lights, Richard's face looked

somewhat startled, but Adriana spoke to him in Italian, letting her eyes run over his elegant frame.

'Just like old times!' Carl's voice was dangerously close to breaking into laughter.

Richard was now introducing Jenny and Alix was sure something was about to happen, only Adriana smiled.

'A lioness might smile like that,' Carl observed.

Beatrice Halford hurried up, beginning to understand why Alix was looking nervous, getting a protective arm around young Jenny.

'Thank you, Richard darling, for playing so beautifully. Now both of you must meet my guests.'

An hour and a half later, Alix turned to confront Adriana, black eyes glittering like live coals.

'Damn him. *Damn* him!' she muttered through her gritted teeth.

So much for reconciliation! Alix stared at her, then took her arm. 'Please, Adriana, you've been so wonderful up until now.'

'I could see you were much relieved,' Adriana hissed. 'He must be *insane* to bring that child here.'

'Not if you knew why,' Alix murmured, and sought the privacy of the heavy velvet drapery.

'*Tell* me!' Adriana demanded with a fierce look that would have shattered anyone else.

'Even if you heard it, Adriana, what would it do? Give you pause. Make you listen. You can't afford to let history repeat itself—not if you want Richard.'

'And I *do*.' Adriana pressed a hand to her beautiful,

creamy bosom. 'Richard is my sun, my moon, my life. Together we are immortal!'

'Then why do you make his life a misery with your jealousy?'

Adriana drew back and broke into Italian.

'I'm sorry, I don't understand your beautiful language.'

'*You*, little girl, who *are* you?' Adriana looked furious and wronged.

'Someone who wants to help you,' Alix answered, quiet and unsmiling. 'Make a scene tonight and you've said goodbye to Richard. I'm certain he still loves you, but he's standing at the crossroads.'

'He's *indecent*!' Adriana exclaimed.

'You have no real rival.' Alix clenched her hands together and kept on talking quietly. 'If he thrives on female admiration, you'd better turn a blind eye to it. After all, you told me yourself it all happens under your eye. Maybe that's as much of an affair as he needs. Maybe he's always trying to rouse *you*. He could even get his kicks that way. Jenny doesn't count, all the pretty women he finds amusing. It's you that makes him writhe in pain. When you came on stage tonight, he said you looked glorious!'

'Of course!' Adriana took the compliment straightforwardly. 'I have no equal as Violetta.' She was looking at Richard across the room, dark head thrown back, the silver wings so distinguished. As his wife, she felt entitled to murder him.

'He's testing you, Adriana,' Alix said gently.

'Villain! Philanderer!' Adriana didn't appear to be

listening. Such a welter of emotion emanated from her body the air was thick with it.

'Ah well!' Alix sighed. 'If you can't see your way to common sense. I rather wanted to see you and Richard reunited. Richard wants it in his secret heart, but you, Adriana, won't let it happen.' She went to move away, but Adriana caught at her hand.

'Dear child, I am such a bitch!'

'Oh, *no*!' Alix shook her shining blonde head.

'I am,' Adriana insisted. 'I have been all my life. If you had only witnessed all the wrongs Richard has done me, you would understand.'

'I *do* understand,' Alix said feelingly, and she did. 'The thing is, you can't feel for anyone else what you feel for Richard. You *want* him. You want to remarry him.'

'We are still married in the sight of God,' Adriana pointed out piously.

'Then you must be the magnanimous one. Forget your natural resentments. See, Richard is looking across at us now. He's waiting for something important to happen, good or bad. Play your cards right, Adriana, and he'll go back to America with you as your husband.'

'Do you think so?' Adriana's nails bit deeply into Alix's soft flesh.

'I'm sure of it.'

'It is what I want,' Adriana said in a deeply moving tone. 'I shall never trust him, which is just as well, but it is no life without him.'

'Tell him that.'

'We should have you to live with us,' Adriana said, 'then you could keep the peace.'

What a life! Alix smiled, grateful that Carl was moving towards them.

'It's been a wonderful evening,' he said smilingly, 'but I think, darling, we'd better go. I'm taking you out to the house in the morning, remember?'

'This house that Alix's father built?' Adriana beamed on both of them. 'The house you are always talking about?'

'Of course.' Carl took Adriana's hand and kissed it. 'You were unforgettable tonight.'

'I am a difficult woman,' Adriana said gently, her full mouth curving in a wry smile. 'I shall thank you both for your great help by giving you the most in-depth portrait of my life.'

'Perfect!' smiled Carl. 'Any time you like. We're entirely at your disposal.'

'Now I shall go to my husband,' Adriana told them. 'Ignoring all his little faults. How shall this Jenny get home?'

'We'll drop her off on the way.'

When they finally left the party, Adriana and Richard only had eyes for each other.

Alix slept late in the morning and by the time she was dressed, Carl had arrived and he and Peter were talking together out on the balcony.

'Hi!' It was a very offhand greeting for a newly engaged girl to her fiancé, but Carl didn't appear to find anything amiss.

'You look a little tired.' He stood up and kissed her cheek, pulling a chair out for her at the same time.

'I am.' She stretched her arms above her head. 'I kept dreaming about Richard and Adriana. They were having a terrible fight.'

'Who cares!' said Peter, bored with the whole thing. 'If they hate one another so much why did they get married in the first place?'

'Life teaches us all lessons,' Carl laughed. 'So far as I'm concerned, they can work it all out for themselves. All we need now is the interview and pictures.' As he was speaking, his black eyes were running over Alix's lovely pale face and slender body. This morning she wore leggy cotton slacks with a body-hugging little T-shirt and she looked very young and delectable.

'Do you think they'll really stay together?' she looked up at Carl suddenly to ask.

'God knows!' He shrugged his powerful shoulders.

'You know, Sis,' Peter said a little anxiously, 'those two are wearing you out.'

'Don't worry,' Carl put his hand on Peter's head, 'they're going home.'

'We're only presuming they are,' said Alix. 'No one really knows.'

'Want to bet?' Carl gave her a brilliant sidelong glance.

'I don't think I could stand it if they broke up again.' Unexpectedly she blushed. If Richard made love half as well as Carl, last night would have been a total triumph.

'I'm sorry I'm not coming with you,' said Peter, looking over the balcony to see if he could catch sight of Rusty's father's car. He and Rusty were playing in a tennis tournament and it was unthinkable they should miss it.

'Never mind. We'll take you on our next visit.'

'Life is funny, isn't it?' Peter looked a little startled at his own thought. 'I never thought we'd see our house again. Alix and I couldn't even bear to drive past.' For an instant there were tears in his eyes, but he blinked them away fiercely. 'We really needed you, Carl.'

Carl, apparently, was not afraid of emotion, for he caught the boy to him and hugged him. 'I know I needed *you*!'

'Tell me,' Alix asked, a golden haze before her own eyes, 'do I figure in any of this?'

'What a stupid question!' Peter broke into a gleeful laugh. 'Say, it's Rusty! Where's my racket?'

After they had seen him off, the unit was very quiet.

'You don't want to go, do you?' Carl asked gravely, regarding her with sombre eyes.

'It's wonderful for Peter.' She answered him in a voice that didn't seem like her own.

'Peter, of course.'

'After all, Carl,' she swung around to challenge him, 'you know I don't love you.'

'Don't *say* that!' Some deep emotion flared in his eyes.

'I don't.' She stood there staring at him, feeling smothered as always by his powerful masculinity.

'But you're smart enough to realise there are other important considerations in marriage?'

'I want to love you,' she said, starting tremble.

'Don't get upset.' He moved towards her, but she

stopped him with an uplifted hand.

'Don't touch me, Carl. I can't *think* when you touch me.'

'No wonder you and your Guy got on so beautifully together!'

'What's that supposed to mean?' She flushed under the brilliant intelligence in his eyes.

'You're frightened to love, Alix. You're frightened to let yourself go. There's something not ladylike about it.'

'Don't you go psychoanalysing me,' she said jerkily. 'I said from the start, we're not compatible.'

'So you want to call this marriage off, Alix, my love, my crazy, crazy love.'

She hesitated, a little thrown by his mockery. 'Do *you?*'

'It's all of ten o'clock,' he said. 'I'm going out to see our house.'

There were tears in her eyes, but for the first time he ignored them.

'Why do you want me, Carl?' She seemed surprised he did.

'To improve myself.' There was a dangerous glint in his eye. 'You're right about reminding me of a fairytale princess. Beauty and the Beast.'

'You're not a beast!' she protested, a little shocked at his harshness.

'Really?' He walked across to the sliding glass doors that led out on to the balcony and shut them. 'When have you ever thought to discover what I am?'

'Are you sure you even like me?' She looked up a little timidly at his tough, dark face.

'It's about time you acted like an adult. You can advise other people on how to live their lives. Richard told me, *and* Adriana. Bring a little wisdom to your own.'

In the car Alix didn't know if he was being very intelligent or intimidating her. Both considerations kept her silent.

'I saw young Sally the other day,' he said, after a long pause.

'Oh?' That silly little thing! her nerves screamed. She couldn't bear the thought of Sally in Carl's arms. The meaningless, brazen sex.

'She's pregnant.'

'I'm not surprised.'

'You sound as bad as Gary. She's not a bad little kid. She asked me to remember her to you.'

'Who did she marry?' Alix asked. 'Or isn't she married?'

'If she was as smart as you, Alix, or had the benefit of your upbringing, she wouldn't be in the mess she's in now.'

'Oh.' She could feel the contrition beating in her throat. 'I'm sorry. I suppose you helped her out?'

'I gave her a little money, yes. Directed her to some people who could help. At least she's got the guts to want to keep her child.'

'And you admired that?' She glanced at his taut profile.

'Of course. She'll make it and she'll love her child the way a mother should. She'll even learn from her bitter lesson. She'll never be so silly or so careless again.'

'She told me once she was having an affair with you,' said Alix in a low voice, her head bent.

'You believed her?' He clicked his tongue in contempt.

'I did then. She told me how you took her . . . to your apartment . . . she told me. . . .

'Oh, shut up,' he said harshly. 'I thought you had more sense.'

'But then you don't know me either!' she cried emotionally. 'I don't want to go with you, Carl. I don't want to go at all.'

'Sit still!' he said sharply, and flicked the locking device. 'Peter's right, this business with Kaufmann has been getting to you.'

Alix gave an involuntary little moan and put her hands over her ears. She was terribly on edge, and the worst part was that she wanted him to take her in his arms and make her dizzy with kisses. It was savage, the mad rush of desire. Savage and unwanted and impossible to control.

Carl must have been feeling it too, for he put out his hand and ran it yearningly over her breast. 'You know what's really wrong with you, don't you?' he said tensely.

She leant her head back against the headrest and closed her eyes. Did frustration make one restless and weepy? Did she simply want to go to bed with him? A warmblooded woman like everyone else?

They never exchanged another word until they reached the house, then Alix sat up, eyes unnaturally bright. It was only the second time she had seen it since the terrible day she and Peter had moved out.

'It's only been empty two days,' Carl said.

Alix scarcely heard him, feeling so sensitive she was open to any kind of wounding. The house was even more beautiful than she remembered it, the work of a highly sophisticated and intelligent human being. Her father.

Carl sat in the car and watched her as she jumped out of the car and moved across the velvet grass to the wide flight of steps that led to the entrance. She looked like a girl in a trance, her golden hair flying. The whole rear of the house opened out on to the water, a shimmering deep blue, shades deeper than the cloudless sky above them.

After a minute, because he had the key, Carl got out. Alix was poised on the top of the flight of steps like a bird, uncertain in which direction to fly. When he got nearer he noticed how distraught her eyes were; wide and shining, transparent in colour.

'Alix,' he said gently, and took firm hold of her hand.

'Why do you want to live here, Carl?' she asked him in a breathless undertone.

'Because you belong here.'

Stripped of furniture the house should have lost a great deal of character, but it didn't. It was truly a work of art, a great sculpture. Light poured through the skylights and the high horizontal windows and sparkled through the stained glass that had been used like jewels.

Alix's young face was totally absorbed, yet curiously still as though she were listening to sounds from a yesteryear. They walked through all the free flowing spaces of the ground floor with its two wings, then they climbed the broad flight of stairs to the master bedroom suite. It had a wonderful sloping copper ceiling and an uninterrupted and very private view of the shimmering blue water.

'Daddy had a lot of financial problems when he was building this house,' Alix told Carl. 'But he was determined to finish it, for *us*. Everything in it is of the very highest quality. He came up with all kinds of revolutionary ideas, ideas other architects have since copied. It didn't seem important he didn't leave us much money. He left *this*!' Her beautifully formed tender mouth started to quiver. 'Life is cruel!'

'It's also a celebration,' he said quietly, and drew her back against him. 'You have wonderful memories of your mother and father, Alix, memories that will stay with you all your life. All over this city are the beautiful houses your father built. Nothing is going to destroy that. From what I've seen of Peter's work, he's inherited a great deal of talent. Together we can offer him stability and security, a good future. I count it a privilege.'

'I believe you do.' Her eyes had a distant look.

They stood there, both of them, Carl's arms around her, looking out over the water. 'When are you going to be my bride, Alix?' he murmured against her temple.

What am I afraid of? she wondered yet again. He was so much more than she had ever imagined; in spirit and mind. In *body*. She began to tremble and he turned her round in his arms.

'Tell me now.'

He had acquired a way of looking at her lately; deeply, searchingly, penetrating to her very soul. She thought in bitter amusement that she really did love him after all, and at the strange smile on her mouth Carl caught her savagely to him, overpowering her with his strength, crushing her mouth turbulently under his. He had never been beset by such fury, and he picked her up in a storm of passion, never for a moment thinking of rejecting what he had always wanted.

All at once Alix wanted it too, and they were lying on the thickly piled geometrically patterned carpet, both breathing deeply in a blaze of emotion. 'I want you *now*,' he said huskily, in a kind of appalled voice. 'I'll go mad soon.' The black eyes were full of a determined passion, the whites brilliantly white.

'Tell me you care for me.'

'Alix, for God's sake!' He lowered his head, until it rested between her breasts.

She sighed deeply, feeling the answering tremble in his body, the mounting sexual urgency. One hand came up under her T-shirt to caress her body, moving higher. It was the sort of thing she craved for, and she bent to kiss the top of his dark head, thinking in the space of a single second that it was only defiance that prevented her from telling him she was hopelessly in love with him; would love him more and more every day. Carl was a man to discover, past, present, future, everything!

'My beautiful girl!' His hands cupped her breasts almost reverently, and she felt the sensation surging through every inch of her skin.

'Make love to me.' Her head was spinning, her

body totally reckless. She could see the excitement in his eyes, the loss of control. Carl, in her power.

His strong arms wrapped right around her and he half covered her slender body with his own, unerringly finding her mouth.

'Carl,' she whispered soundlessly, 'I love you.' Incredible. She had said it.

In the silence of the house, a woman's voice echoed up from the ground floor.

'Carl? Yoo-hoo . . . anyone there?'

'Great God!' Carl's voice came up from deep within his throat. He didn't want to move, but he had to move in a hurry. He lifted himself away from Alix, buttoning his shirt and tucking it back into the waistband.

'Did you tell her you'd be here?' Alix asked in a strange voice.

'You know better,' he frowned, and loped away. 'Stay there. I'll be back.'

Not to me you won't! Alix was consumed with jealousy and doubt. Would Barbra be a constant visitor? In this new liberated era anything went.

She stood up dizzily, aware of the unsatiated ache in her body. Barbra Goulden was a determined woman and she had made no bones about wanting Carl. If she wasn't her rival as a suitable wife, she was a possibility as an extra-marital affair. In the magazine business, nothing was shocking news. She and Adriana were really throwbacks to another age.

What age? she thought, almost losing her footing hurrying down the steps of the children's wing.

She could see Carl and Barbra easily. They were now standing at the front of the house, Barbra's snappy little red Porsche drawn up alongside the Jaguar.

What was he telling her? she thought. Thank God she couldn't hear. She couldn't stand it. Was there anything in the world called true love? Of course there was. Her mother and father had found it. She didn't feel ridiculous hiding. The grounds were big; Carl would never find her.

Of course she could give him the benefit of the doubt. Sheer effrontery had brought Barbra here. She was a business woman, a real go-getter. Probably she had all sorts of plans drawn up for furnishing the house. Alix eased herself down on to the grass, taking the pressure off her arms.

If Barbra hadn't turned up, she would now have passed through the most transfiguring experience of her life. What a fool she was, to believe what she wanted to believe. Carl didn't love her. She could just give him what he wanted—a highly respectable-looking young wife, essential for a would-be politician. The Senator had been on the phone to him several times last week. He was a mystery man, Carl. She could never hope to fathom him.

Barbra's laugh tinkled in the brilliant air, and Alix's poignant young face took on an expression of pain and distaste. Should she go forward and speak?

Hello there, Barbra. Carl has had so many girl-friends, you know, but he's going to marry *me*! A declaration of war. *No.* It simply wasn't her style. Wouldn't you think he'd get rid of her? After all, he had another day planned.

Just as Alix moved a little gingerly, for she was cramped, Barbra suddenly threw her arms up around Carl's neck and kissed him resoundingly.

'That does it!' Alix said aloud, thinking she would die of betrayal. She was shaking so badly, she fell back on the grass. She really understood now what Adriana had meant when she spoke of the wrongs that had been done her. A woman was a fool to expect fidelity from any man.

She lay there until the Porsche had gone and she could see Carl move away up the steps, then she leapt to her feet and streaked diagonally across the grass. There were plenty of places to hide in the landscaped grounds. She never wanted to see Carl again, or any other man for that matter.

After a full minute, her brain won. This was so stupid and undignified. Trees arched above her, dark green and beautiful, a breeze stirring the leaves. One thing was clear: she had to make a decision. Carl had said he wanted her, but he had never said he loved her. She sat down on the grass and sighed at herself. She had never said she loved *him*. Not aloud. She gave a funny little laugh, a wry, despairing laugh. How extraordinary the one person who could show her how much she loved Carl was Barbra. She could see now why Sally had invented all those stories, to shock her. She was so easily shocked.

When he found her, she was still lying on the grass and he pulled her into his arms, stroking back her tumbled hair.

'Oh, Alix,' he said helplessly. Strong, positive, ruthless Carl.

'I'm such a fool!' Her silvery eyes were very sad.

'Ah, who isn't?' He traced the line of her cheek with a quiet, sweet tenderness. 'But there's a lesson in it. We should say what we mean.'

'What did she want?' she asked.

'Work. She runs a business, remember?'

'I don't know whether she should be allowed to kiss the clients.'

'It was all my fault,' he said lightly. 'I gave her a job.'

'*No!*' Alix had sorted herself out sufficiently to feel angry. 'How can you let her do my job? *Our* job!'

'So you're going to marry me, then?' He tipped up her chin to stare down into her eyes.

'Yes.' Now it was truly final.

She expected him to kiss her, his dark eyes had grown so brilliant, but he held back. 'Because of Peter?'

'Something even more important, because I love you.' She put her fingers up and traced the line of his mouth. '*Please* don't let Barbra do the house.'

'There you go again,' he said gently, 'jumping to conclusions. How could I possibly let Barbra do such a thing? Stop and think for a minute.'

'I didn't think you would.'

'She'll be quite happy with the Carrington job.'

'Oh,' she sighed softly, a delicate flush in her cheeks. 'You're good to a lot of people, aren't you?'

Carl moved abruptly, lowering her to the grass, his

arms sliding under her while he supported himself on his elbows. 'Do you want a church wedding?'

'Yes.' Why wouldn't he kiss her, when she could feel little arrowheads of flame?

'Where do you want to go for our honeymoon?'

'Oh, *anywhere*!' What did it matter so long as they were both together?

His black eyes were resting on her flushed, impatient face. She looked very beautiful and unmistakably wanting to be kissed.

'Tell me you love me again.'

'Oh, why are you *talking* like this?' She lifted both her arms in a fever of frustration and pulled his head down to her. 'I love you. I love you. I've done nothing else but fight it, but I do. . . .'

He rained kisses on her, such a mixture of tenderness and violence it seemed he was intent on inflicting pain. Only she loved it, revelled in his strength and passion. Tears slid along her cheeks and her hair was all around them, golden and silky and scented with grass and shampoo. This was beautiful beyond belief, and it was only a little part of what they would experience together.

'I've meant to have you from the instant I laid eyes on you,' Carl told her.

'Why?' she murmured between kisses, feeling her whole body shivering with delight.

'At the very beginning because I wanted you for a lover. You're so beautiful, everything I want in a woman. After a little while, that wasn't enough. I wanted you—*Alix*. Heart and body and mind.' He spoke a little harshly as though he had difficulty saying the words. 'I *love* you—all of you. I want you for my wife, the mother of my children. For always.'

'You've never said that before, have you?' she said wonderingly.

'No.' He caught her fingers and put the tips between his teeth. 'Total commitment has always filled me with panic, but not with you. You're in my blood.'

'Oh, Carl!' she said in a shaken whisper. 'It's such a responsibility, your love.'

'Perhaps that's *it*, darling.' He kissed the palm of her hand and she closed her eyes in rapture. 'Love is responsibility. Holding another person's life and happiness in the palm of your hand.'

'I'll be everything you want,' she said intensely. 'I'll love and adore. . . .'

'And obey?' Carl lowered his head and kissed her throat.

'I see no reason to obey.'

'You'll just want to.'

'Yes.' Alix opened her eyes, startled at the love and curious humility in his expression. It gave her a tremendous rush of elation. 'Would it inconvenience you, darling, if we got married at the end of the month?'

Masquerade
Historical Romances

*Intrigue
excitement
romance*

THE RELUCTANT MATCH
by Polly Meyrick

Sophie modelled her conduct on that of the heroines
of her favourite novels. But not even Lenore, in *The
Prisoner of the Vampire,* was ordered to marry an old,
balding stranger! So Sophie ran away to London and
met the mysterious Mr Fanshawe, who looked like a
hero and behaved like a villain . . .

GLEN OF FROST
by Belinda Grey

Fiona Seidhe Maclaren was caught in a bitter struggle
when she fell in love with her cousin Lachlan. Forced
to marry his bastard brother, Jamie, she became the
prize in a blood feud that reached its climax at the
Battle of Culloden, where brother fought brother.
Could her love survive such bitter hatred?

Look out for these titles in your local paperback shop from
10th April 1981

The Mills & Boon Rose is the Rose of Romance

Every month there are ten new titles to choose from — ten new stories about people falling in love, people you want to read about, people in exciting, far-away places. Choose Mills & Boon. It's your way of relaxing:

April's titles are:

THE STORM EAGLE *by Lucy Gillen*
In other circumstances Chiara would have married Campbell Roberts. But he had not consulted her. And now wild horses wouldn't make her accept him!

SECOND-BEST BRIDE *by Margaret Rome*
Angie would never have guessed how the tragedy that had befallen Terzan Helios would affect her own life . . .

WOLF AT THE DOOR *by Victoria Gordon*
Someone had to win the battle of wills betwwen Kelly Barnes and her boss Grey Scofield, in their Rocky Mountains camp . . .

THE LIGHT WITHIN *by Yvonne Whittal*
Now that Roxy might recover her sight, the misunderstanding between her and Marcus Fleming seemed too great for anything to bridge it . . .

SHADOW DANCE *by Margaret Way*
If only her new job assignment had helped Alix to sort out the troubled situation between herself and her boss Carl Danning!

SO LONG A WINTER *by Jane Donnelly*
'You'll always be too young and I'll always be too old,' Matt Hanlon had told Angela five years ago. Was the situation any different now?

NOT ONCE BUT TWICE *by Betty Neels*
Christina had fallen in love at first sight with Professor Adam ter Brandt. But hadn't she overestimated his interest in her?

MASTER OF SHADOWS *by Susanna Firth*
The drama critic Max Anderson had wrecked Vanessa's acting career with one vicious notice, and then Vanessa became his secretary . . .

THE TRAVELLING KIND *by Janet Dailey*
Charley Collins knew that she must not get emotionally involved with Shad Russell. But that was easier said than done . . .

ZULU MOON *by Gwen Westwood*
In order to recover from a traumatic experience Julie went to Zululand, and once again fell in love with a man who was committed elsewhere . . .

If you have difficulty in obtaining any of these books from your local paperback retailer, write to:

Mills & Boon Reader Service
P.O. Box 236, Thornton Road, Croydon, Surrey, CR9 3RU.

Doctor Nurse Romances

and April's
stories of romantic relationships behind the scenes
of modern medical life are:

CHILDREN'S NURSE
by Kathryn Blair

Nurse Linda Gréy travels to Portugal to look after
four-year old Jacinto but her modern ideas meet with
strong opposition from the boy's father, the handsome
Marquez de Filano.

MAJOR MIKE
by Hazel Fisher

When under Major Mike's command at the Territorial
Army camp, Nurse Lisa Hilton tries hard to ignore his
sarcastic comments, only to find she is haunted by
the Major's piercing dark eyes . . .

Order your copies today from your local paperback retailer

The Mills & Boon Rose is the Rose of Romance

THE McIVOR AFFAIR *by Margaret Way*
How could Marnie kill this feeling of attraction that was growing between her and the hateful Drew McIvor, whom her stepmother had cheated?

ICE IN HIS VEINS *by Carole Mortimer*
Jason Earle was a cold, unfeeling man. Yet, given the right circumstances, Eden could like him altogether too much!

A HAUNTING COMPULSION *by Anne Mather*
Despite the bitterness Rachel Williams felt about Jaime Shard, she accepted to spend Christmas with his parents. But Jaime would be there too . . .

DEVIL'S CAUSEWAY *by Mary Wibberley*
Why did Maria have to complicate the situation by falling in love with Brand Cordell, who was angry and bitter about the whole thing?

AUTUMN IN APRIL *by Essie Summers*
Gaspard MacQueen hoped Rosamond would come and settle in New Zealand, but his grandson Matthieu had *quite* another view of the situation!

THE INTERLOPER *by Robyn Donald*
It was the hard Dane Fowler whom Meredith really feared. All the more so, because of her unwilling love for him . . .

BED OF ROSES *by Anne Weale*
Was her husband Drogo Wolfe's involvement with his 'close friend' Fiona turning Annis's bed of roses into a bed of thorns?

BEYOND THE LAGOON *by Marjorie Lewty*
When her deception was discovered Gideon North's opinion of Susan French would hardly be improved. Why did she care so much?

SUMMER OF THE RAVEN *by Sara Craven*
Rowan was stuck with Carne Maitland, the one man she really wanted – and one who was totally out of reach.

ON THE EDGE OF LOVE *by Sheila Strutt*
Dulcie fell in love with the cold Jay Maitland – only to find that his coldness didn't apply to the beautiful Corinne Patterson!

If you have difficulty in obtaining any of these books from your local paperback retailer, write to:

Mills & Boon Reader Service
P.O. Box 236, Thornton Road, Croydon, Surrey, CR9 3RU.
Available May 1981

SAVE TIME, TROUBLE & MONEY!
By joining the exciting NEW...

 **Mills & Boon**
Romance CLUB

WITH all these EXCLUSIVE BENEFITS for every member

NOTHING TO PAY! MEMBERSHIP IS FREE TO REGULAR READERS!

IMAGINE the *pleasure* and *security* of having ALL your favourite *Mills & Boon* romantic fiction delivered right to *your* home, absolutely POST FREE... straight off the press! No waiting! No more disappointments! All this PLUS all the latest news of *new books* and *top-selling authors* in your own monthly MAGAZINE... PLUS *regular* big CASH SAVINGS... PLUS lots of wonderful strictly-limited, *members-only* SPECIAL OFFERS! All these exclusive benefits can be *yours* – right NOW – simply by joining the exciting NEW *Mills & Boon* ROMANCE CLUB. Complete and post the coupon below for FREE full-colour leaflet. It costs nothing. HURRY!

No obligation to join unless you wish!

FREE CLUB MAGAZINE Packed with *advance* news of latest titles and authors

Exciting offers of **FREE BOOKS** For club members ONLY

Lots of fabulous **BARGAIN OFFERS** –many at **BIG CASH SAVINGS**

FREE FULL-COLOUR LEAFLET!
CUT OUT CUT OUT COUPON BELOW AND POST IT TODAY!

To: **MILLS & BOON READER SERVICE, P.O. Box No 236, Thornton Road, Croydon, Surrey CR9 3RU, England.** WITHOUT OBLIGATION to join, please send me FREE details of the exciting NEW *Mills & Boon* ROMANCE CLUB and of all the exclusive benefits of membership.

Please write in BLOCK LETTERS below

NAME (Mrs/Miss) ....

ADDRESS ....

CITY/TOWN ....

COUNTY/COUNTRY.......................... POST/ZIP CODE....................

Readers in South Africa and Zimbabwe please write to: P.O. BOX 1872, Johannesburg, 2000. S. Africa